S INKING

INKING

**A Story of the Disaster Which Took Place
at the Blyvooruitzicht Mine, Far West Rand,
on 3 August 1964**

*(Being a History, Romance, Allegory, Prophecy, Survey,
Domestic Drama – and None of the Above)*

by

MICHAEL CAWOOD GREEN

with

A Full Critical Apparatus
An Afterword by Michael Green
And Selected Songs by the Author

PENGUIN BOOKS

PENGUIN BOOKS

Published by the Penguin Group
27 Wrights Lane, London W8 5TZ, England
Viking Penguin, a division of Penguin Books USA Inc, 375
Hudson Street, New York, New York 10014, USA
Penguin Books Australia Ltd, Ringwood, Victoria, Australia
Penguin Books Canada Ltd, 10 Alcorn Avenue, Toronto,
Ontario, Canada M4V 3B2
Penguin Books (NZ) Ltd, 182-190 Wairau Road, Auckland 10,
New Zealand
Penguin Books South Africa (Pty) Ltd, Pallinghurst Road,
Parktown, South Africa 2193

Penguin Books South Africa (Pty) Ltd, Registered Offices:
20 Woodlands Drive, Woodmead, Sandton, South Africa 2128

First published by Penguin Books South Africa (Pty) Ltd 1997

ISBN 0 140 58790 X

Typeset in 10.5 on 13 point Melior
Front cover: The Image Bank
Back cover: *Die Transvaler*
Author photograph: Carole Lynch
Printed and bound by The Rustica Press, Old Mill Road, Ndabeni,
Western Cape
D5808

For both Données

. . . a dispersed fragment, reaching us by chance, of an obscure shadowy world that can be reconnected to our own history only by an arbitrary act. That culture has been destroyed. To respect its residue of unintelligibility that resists any attempt at analysis does not mean succumbing to a foolish fascination for the exotic and incomprehensible. It is simply taking note of a historical mutilation of which, in a certain sense, we ourselves are the victims.

Carlo Ginzburg, *The Cheese and the Worms: The Cosmos of a Sixteenth-Century Miller*

With thanks to:

Jurgens Hamman for the initial exposure and technical advice;
various members of the Elandsrand community for their information and interest;
Stephen Gray, Breyten Breytenbach, and Michael Chapman for their encouragement;
Alison Lowry for her belief in the project;
and
Leon de Kock for support of both the most inspirational and practical kind.

CONTENTS

SECTION 1: PAST
SINKING

The Text-Book Version		3
1.	Older Than Time	4
2.	Premonition	13
3.	The Event: As John Coetzee Would Have It	14
4.	Falling (Hettie's Love Song)	16
5.	From Event To Structure: The MacMasters	18
6.	After the Fact	19
7.	A Period of Silence	20
8.	A Washing Machine at the End of the World	23
9.	Marianne, Warm in Blankets	25
10.	I Am the Only Ghost	27
11.	Juvenilia	31
12.	The End of the First Person: An Introduction	32
13.	From Structure To Event: Willie Britz	36
14.	Father Like Water	39
15.	Ventriloquist Without a Dummy: Voices for Workers	45
16.	Call Me Delene	48
17.	Johannes's Love Song	50
18a.	Translation: *Mise-en-Abyme*	51
18b.	Freely, From the Afrikaans, based on the poem 'Skagbodem van die Myn en 3.2 Pompstasie' by Pieter G. Mocke	55
19.	The Big Picture	62
20.	Graves: Hettie's Epigraphy	64
21.	Apophrades: Or, a Beginner's Modernism	70

SECTION 2: MEDIATION
APPENDICES

APPENDIX 1: MARGINALIA

1.	The Art of Poetry	83
2.	Failures With Metaphor	84
3.	A Materialist Aesthetics	85
4.	Ethics	86
5.	Autobiography	88
6.	Fourth of August, 1994	89

APPENDIX 2: SOURCES
Extracts from 'Towards a Note on the Sources
of *Sinking*' by Donnée Phelps   93

APPENDIX 3: DEFINITIONS
Some Working Definitions   101

APPENDIX 4: COMMENTARY
Autolycusthony and the Black Hole:
Cawood Green's *Sinking* as 'None of the Above'
by Alan Murray Charles   109

SECTION 3: PRESENT
AFTERWORD: THE SECRET HISTORY
OF *SINKING* by Michael Green   119
Including, in no particular order, observations on:
songwriting, answering-machine etiquette, suicide,
painting, baths, greeting cards, art history, morality,
creativity, nudity, autobiography, poetry, nationalism,
genre, names, family history, murder, literary history,
detection, ghosts, local history, executions, the life of
the author, grammar, and the future; supplemented
with

The Songs:

1:	The Soldier's Got A Name	143
2:	Three Verses For M	145
3:	John Vorster Square	147
4:	Berlin, 1931	149
5:	An Old South African Love Song, Or, Sarie Marais Revisited	151
6:	Lili Marleen (Again)	153
7:	Casual Violence	155
8:	Heroine Goes Home, Bleeding	157
9:	Untitled	159

SECTION 1: PAST

SINKING

THE TEXT-BOOK VERSION

> *Earth is an amalgam*
> *of hatreds stone and love,*
> *of clay and iron hopes.*
> Rui de Matos, 'Geology Lesson'

A sinkhole is a subsidence which appears suddenly, and sometimes with catastrophic consequences, as a cylindrical and steep-sided hole in the ground. It is usually, but not always, circular in plan, and may be up to 125 metres wide and 50 metres deep. If the dimensions exceed 45 metres in diameter and 30 metres in depth, it is regarded as a large sinkhole.

....

3 August 1964
A sinkhole . . . appeared in a mining village at Blyvooruitzig Mine (Oberholzer Compartment) in the middle of the night and claimed the lives of the Oosthuizen family of five as their house suddenly dropped more than 30 m. Three other houses which were situated on the edge of the initial collapse also fell in within a short period of time as the sides of the sinkhole caved in, their occupants making dramatic escapes. Subsequent enquiry revealed that there had been leakage from water pipes in the area where the sinkhole appeared.

A.B.A. Brink, *Engineering Geology of Southern Africa: The First 2 000 Million Years of Geological Time* (Pretoria: Building Publications, 1979).

1.   OLDER THAN TIME

> *... this land is not the sweet home that it looks,*
> *Nor its peace the historical calm of a site*
> *Where something was settled once and for all ...*
> W.H. Auden, 'In Praise of Limestone', 1948

Anyone would have built a house here,
Laid out a village even,
As the Mine did.
Nothing really nestles in the Western Transvaal,
But if this ridge
(Like the others that break this high, bare expanse
Pressed against *more sky than you have ever seen*)
Was too rocky for such comfort,
Its casually protective arm
Still made a pleasant corner
On the bare sandy tract west of the Mine –
So, Westdene, our home of a hundred or so houses,
Tin-roofed red-brick green-doored and framed house
Neatly neighbouring the other
Tin-roofed red-brick green-doored and framed houses
That are the share of the wealth
Squeezed out of earth and men
That is due to our
Rank and race.
And if, now, the perspective
Provided by this position

Is dominated by the shine and angles
Of the steel and corrugated iron
That is the surface symbol
Of Blyvooruitzicht's Number Two shaft,
Still, it is a happy prospect indeed
For those of us who live to extract a living
Out of that which supports us,
Whose dependence is
Poised
Between the impenetrable
And the need to penetrate.

This situation, however,
Finds its order
In another arrangement
Infinitely older and more substantial
Than the relations of its surface;
And the reasons behind choosing this place,
Behind the aesthetics of perspective
And the demands of practicality,
Did not take into account all the laws
Governing this place.
These are simple (when understood)
But more important,
Unnegotiable.

For example,
This ridge is here because it is quartz
And quartzite does not easily erode;

And the flatness that it embraces
Is flat because it is yielding dolomite.
This is why, in Plomer's Transvaal morning,
'Shoulders of quartz protruded from the hill
Like sculpture half unearthed';
No less in ours, and
This much, more prosaically,
We knew – even more,
That the plain face of dolomite,
The tempting domesticity of its
Scoured surface smoothness,
Is eaten out from within by conflicts
Older than poetry,
Older even than the politics
That made the year in which Auden wrote
His poem in praise of dolomite's near-relative
So significant for us.
Like limestone, dolomite *dissolves in water*,
So holes,
Eaten out by water,
And now filled with water,
Form in it too *a secret system of caves and conduits*
That in places (and this we did not know)
Is all that supports a surface
Seemingly secure enough
For the weight of our efforts
To sink through this
Mild medium of soft moist stone.
For us dolomite contained no geology lesson,

No extended metaphor for *a faultless love*
Or the life to come;
No, for us it was of significance only
For its position between us
And the auriferous conglomerates
Beneath.

And who can blame us
For ignoring dolomite?
Here under the Far West Rand,
Under the bland facade of its flatness,
Lurks the temptation of twenty percent
Of the world's gold;
Blyvoor's near neighbour,
We remind those who have not heard of us,
Is West Driefontein,
The largest single producer of gold in the world.
So,
So what if dolomite,
Especially Transvaal dolomite,
Is for you notorious,
If by 1979 Dr Brink in his textbook
Could count thirty eight dead
And point to damage sustained on these
Honey-coloured surfaces
As more severe
Than on any other geological formation
In Southern Africa?
He could only tell you that this sort of thing

'Accelerated in the Far West Rand in the last fifteen years'
Which dates retrospectively
From his first edition, precisely
The innocence of our year
As far as dolomite
Was concerned.

Oh, we knew of sudden subsidences, creating
Cylindrical, steep-sided, and usually circular holes,
But to us these were, at best,
History.
Our forefathers, Voortrekkers,
Called these ridges the Gatsrante
Because of the abundance of karst features to be found
    here;
And anyone could read –
As every one of us did before Smuts
Disappeared up his holism
And betrayed us –
In Deneys Reitz's book
Of how he hid his whole commando from the British
In a hole near where Doornfontein Mine is now.
But that was then,
Local colour for the anecdote
That embroiders the stern tale of how we came to belong
    here,
Details that stitch together our claim to the land
And the unexpected treasure blanketed beneath it.
If you were to leave even history behind,

And talk like the anthropologists of the 'valuable hominid
    remains'
Preserved in the much, much older holes of
Makapansgat, Sterkfontein, Swartkrans,
Well we, for whom time was a thin line between Alpha
    and Omega,
For whom history had to begin and end
To frame the limits of our minds' ability
To contain the cause and effect that explained us,
For whom God marked the outer edge
Of the failure of our imagination,
We, you see, did not believe in
Evolution.

Of course, when that three-storey crusher on West
    Driefontein mine
Disappeared with the morning shift of twenty nine in
    October 1962,
We suffered with our more famous neighbour;
And when Schutte's house became Schutte's Depression
    in 1963
It all came closer home.
And so we began to pay more attention to humble dolomite,
Which kept its network of levels and pressures
A mystery between us and our gold;
We started to inquire, even as we pumped and pumped,
Into the economy of water,
That nuisance factor that dolomite introduced into our
    operations:

Found that certain of those groundwater compartments
Touched our level,
Slept just below the surface,
And reached up for us with tunnels
That remained choked with chert – as long, that is,
As the water table remained static;
Found that what we conceived as our solid base
Could be a bridge,
A delicate span on which,
Poised above eternity,
Clumsily we carried out
Our earthy exercises;
But, and so they comforted us,
Even under these conditions
Our circumstances could be
Strong and stable for a long, long time –
A long, long time, that is,
Unless the water levels
Dropped . . .

We had to keep on pumping, of course;
And so the game began of finding out
What was arch and what was earth –
Which we could only do by thumping the ground
With heavy machinery
And measuring the response;
All well and good,
But the arithmetic only worked if you were above a
    hollow –

Your sums could tell you solid tales
When feet away a drum waited to sing out
Its emptiness.

But still we pumped,
And as the last water trickled away,
Sensitive to the commands of our technology
(While knowing better),
The unforgiving order of things
Called in our debts,
Drew in our surface reality
To fill a deeper logic,
Longer than our chronologies;
Made us submit to a scale upon which
Our sense of duration
Hardly registers,
Those rhythms and patterns of
A history which almost
Stands still.
Those stories older than time
Taught us of borders more significant
Than any we had drawn
In the languages of history, geography, or ethnicity,
And brought these things so crushingly vast
Home to the delicacy
Of domestic detail.

Yes, anyone would have laid out a village here,
Built a house, even

Moved his love – wife, children, all –
Into the shadow of that protective arm,
Never suspecting how it could all slip through,
Soil through his fingers,
Water from his hands.

2.   PREMONITION

This is the long lulled pause
Before history happens . . .
        Tom Paulin, 'Before History'

Cat tip
Toes through the
Dewgrass;
Pussy, pussy, pussy
Foot
Morning may
Break.

3.   THE EVENT: AS JOHN COETZEE WOULD HAVE IT

Few will be able to guess how sad one had to be
in order to resuscitate Carthage.
                    Gustave Flaubert

Rumbled awake, the instincts
Of my time and place assumed thieves.
Always prepared – hand under pillow for my real
    comforter
In these times when our rightful privileges are
    temptations
To those who make them but do not earn them – I
    stormed outside,
Waving my revolver.
There was no one there,
But my weapon felt very small in my hand
When a sigh, as big as the earth exhaling,
Enveloped me. And then a moaning wind wrapped round
    me,
And visible even in the darkness an immense
Dust cloud, drowning fast-dimming street lights,
Loomed up in the place of the next house
In our avenue. Back in our house,
The good Mrs Coetzee was calling
Faint against the groans and gusts of the whole
Earth rearranging itself for sleep,
And so I fled 31st Avenue (lucky street, I always thought,

The same number as our new end-of-May holiday) back
Into the sleepwarm house, still clutching my revolver,
Trying to explain in screams while bundling, shoving,
    carrying
Five staring-eyed fast-asleep children out
In the almost-forgotten (but good Tillie was eight months
    gone
With our next) nakedness of our nightclothes
And into the bakkie.
The streets were a stock car race
As the residents of Westdene forgot their Saturday
    washing and
Polishing, their weekly swearing at some new nick in the
    gloss,
And jockeyed in their various pride-and-joys to the gate,
Bouncing off each other like bumper cars
But still accelerating with the aim common to any race or
    ride –
To get away from it all.

We would creep back later, the first of mile-long queues
To edge their way to the central attraction;
We would nose our cars to the brink later that very night
And play our headlights through the still-rising dust,
And stare, revolvers forgotten now,
Into the emptiness at the heart of us.

4.   FALLING (HETTIE'S LOVE SONG)

(Oosthuizen, Hester C., gebore van der Watt: 10.4.1930 – 3.8.1964)

(For Esthie – who should have been called,
    after her paternal grandmother, Hester.)

I thought it was the sea
Dragging me to the surface,
And away from you;
By the time I began to swim to consciousness
(Registering at some level
That our beach holiday was over,
The shore two days,
An unresolved argument, and
Hundreds of solid earth miles
Away)
I had no way of comprehending
This new reality;
Such fluidity in a foundation
I, a mine worker's wife, after all,
Have often known to dance
Only made sense within the logic
Of the ocean;
Here, though, no lift first
From a rising swell –
Only the drop,
A falling away from the norm, the base, the limit,

The support and measure of all
I know – even the sea,
The crumpled, deathless sea,
Where *the water takes my body without shame,*
And my children dive
To surface again scared and laughing,
And you are always there
To catch me.

I had time,
Moving through the roar like waves,
To untangle myself from you and
Step from our bed,
Fight the floor for purchase
With no legs for this changing element,
And reach a buckling wall,
Where the light switch briefly obeyed
Laws we command by
Submitting ourselves to them;
Blinded at first by the yellow flood
The firm lines of familiarity flickered through into focus
Only to blur quickly into their collapse
When gravity became the only certainty,
Our children a lost hope in another room,
And I heard myself fill the space
Falling away beneath my feet with screaming
As I tried to find my way across all eternity

Back to you.

5.   FROM EVENT TO STRUCTURE:
THE MACMASTERS

On Sunday evening Dulcie MacMaster boasted to
Hester, her neighbour just back from the sea, about
Her strawberries; at two a.m. or thereabouts
Her strawberries had disappeared – her neighbour too.
'Get up, the house is coming down,' screamed Dulcie to
Her Eric, pumping him awake. He scrambled for
The back door, yanked it open and found nothing before
Him. Water burst from walls alive with flames that flew

As tiles popped off around his head. A wind moaned
     through
His shreds of dreams, while bundling children,
     mother-in-law,
And wife through a window, all doors by now jammed
     tight.
Seconds later, all that they owned went down into
The emptiness. MacMaster screamed at officials he saw:
'You said that we were safe. Now you must dig them out!'

6.   AFTER THE FACT

'Oosthuizens Het Vooraf Hul Dood
Gevoel Naderkom'
        Dagbreek, 8 August 1964

Many called it fate,
Said that tears for another week of holiday
Or staying just 'til the Wednesday
That would have saved them
Were forebodings ignored by
A doom-driven father;
But what it comes down to

Is getting the new car
Back in time to be greased
Before work begins.

7.   A PERIOD OF SILENCE

Boom!
Went the sixties:

Our guns
Made the money run
So it was not just Congress
We had to curb
But foreign exchange
And gold reserves;
The working class
Was one thing to crush
But we had, as well,
To halt the rush
Away of capital.

Anglo stepped in
And the state intervened,
Stabilised markets,
Imported machines;

Each ethnic identity
Given a place on the map
To soak up the surplus
Of workers on tap.
Manufacturing exploded,
A ten-year long boom
Echoed through Africa
And gave us the room
To cut off an ARM
Give a Poqo no leg
To stand on, and at
Rivonia, at last,
We cut off the head.

As the silence descended
It was bliss to our ears,
No winds of change here
For years and for years;
'63 was the deadline
For total liberation
Did they think they'd achieve it
With a bomb at a station?
From January to June
Of 1964
203 cases of sabotage;
By '65,
There were no more.

Silence
Fell on the sixties:

And smack in the middle,
The silence yawned
And swallowed whole
The emblem of everything
We did all this for:
A neat little family
In a neat little home
On ground we had conquered
And made our own.

But we spoke through this vacuum –
For twenty more years,
Our teeth become law
To eat up our fears;
Banned other voices,
Silenced each one,
Proclaiming, proscribing

This family our tongue.

(Postscript: The Minister of Mines reported that, as a result of
subsidences, 309 houses were evacuated and 145 demolished in
the Far West Rand in 1966 at a cost of R14 035 700; protective
measures cost a further R4 433 000.)

8. A WASHING MACHINE AT THE END OF THE WORLD

Nothing of importance occurred here, and nothing much of interest, for everybody was wealthy and flourishing.
      Lady Anne Barnard, *Journal of a Tour into the Interior, 1798*

Several of the photographic spreads
Covering Blyvooruitzicht's overnight sensation
Feature it:
A washing machine
Poised inches from the edge of the half-house
Not taken by the 'sinkholegrave'
Which swallowed whole three others,
One complete with a family of five.

This is no subject for the romantic gesture,
Where the earth now, say, like Pringle's sea once,
'Howls for the progeny she nurst,
To swallow them again';
Neither is it cool-blue modern urban stuff
Of Unreal Cities and, say, the buried blooming.
No, this is the place where Viv's *'Wonderful'*
(*'My nerves are bad to-night. Yes, bad'*)
Becomes Ezra's *'Photography?'*,
Where the camera captures a cross-section
Of the ordinary.

The surgery of catastrophe strips away
The invisibility of the familiar,
And the home dissected reveals
For social analysis
The square, enamelled, churning heart
Of our domestic fantasies.

This is why,
Despite Lady Anne's epitaph
For the whole history
Of the middle class,
A family of five
In a hole interests us far more
Than a crusher-crew of twenty nine
Or any number of other more spectacular
Displays of disaster
Involving soldiers, sailors,
Policemen, firemen –
          Workers . . .

It's that damn washing machine that worries us,
So similar to the ones nestled
In our own kitchens or laundries,
Solid consumers of our soiling natures,
Safe as houses.

9.   MARIANNE, WARM IN BLANKETS

(Oosthuizen, Marianne: 7.11.1958 – 3.8.1964)

Marianne,
Warm in blankets,
A six-year old in a shroud,
Says Mamma,
What shape will I take underground?
Why was I born to be planted
To be buried without a sound?
What will I grow into
From this new tummy
Far, far down?

And mother says,
Hush now
Quiet now
Good night
Sleep tight
Pull the ground around you,
Safe and snug
All life long.

What were we,
What would you have been
Up there
In 1964?

Marianne,
Warm in blankets . . .

10. I AM THE ONLY GHOST

> . . . *we passed streams of Native women, their belongings*
> *on their heads, leaving the mining village. They were*
> *servants of evacuees who could no longer employ them.*
> > Sunday Times, 8 August 1964

> *This is my funeral service. We have no ceremonies, only*
> *private dirges and no conclusions, only violent sensations,*
> *each separate. Nothing that has been said meets our case.*
> > Virginia Woolf, *The Waves*

The caption to the newspaper's
Obligatory family portrait
(Rather dated: one
Baby only in the frame; first or
Last? Hettie so young and pretty –
But then she was twenty one with her first,
Only twenty eight with her now six-year old last –
And Johannes, so tie and hanky,
Short back and sides
Proud) read:
Hier is die vader en moeder, Johannes en Hester
    Oosthuizen,
Here is the father and mother, Johannes and Hester
    Oosthuizen,
Met een van hul drie kinders,
With one of their three children

Wat Sondagnag almal in hierdie gat in Carletonville
  verdwyn het,
Who on Sunday night all disappeared into this hole
Saam met hul bediende en vier huise
Along with their servant and four houses.

I am the only ghost
At this funeral of five;
Out of frame,
Out of mind,
I am the mist at the margins
Of the soft-edged family portrait.
Well, was I one of the ones
(One two three four five –
                    Six)
Who, as only the report above would have it,
'Disappeared into the hole'?
None of the others even mention this possibility
Let alone question it.
Although every neat
Red-brick, tin-roofed, green-doored and framed
House (with which I was counted,
When I counted at all)
Had neat outbuildings,
A garage and
Servant's quarters,
We have only heard the burial of Anglias bewailed –
Oh, yes, and that 'the S.P.C.A. is arranging to remove and
Look after all the animals left

Behind by the evacuees';
The servants of evacuees
Must look after themselves
Now they have no-one to look after.

So I am the only ghost at this funeral
Coming in early on Monday morning,
But not early enough –
At six o'clock nearly four hours too late –
To serve or save;
Coming back from leave,
A month who here knows where,
To find my living buried,
My single (Christian) name unspoken
And no other names or places or people available when
After some time
It came to be spoken
As, half-heartedly, some thought to give me a shape, a
    place, a
Meaning in all of this; a meaning
Restricted to relief
At the strong probability
Of my absence
Those crucial four or so
Hours earlier –
A relief that makes my present absence
A little less embarrassing.

So I – the only ghost at this funeral – remain,
As I join the stream of real refugees
(Too scared to claim an identity:
Whose fault is all of this, after all?)
Far less substantial on this solid earth
Than those five (count them) firm bodies
Definitely somewhere,
Even if this is
Precisely eighty feet
Underground.

11.   JUVENILIA

(Oosthuizen, Johannes D.: 16.2.1956 – 3.8.1964)

> *– Dead! says Alf. He is no more dead than you are.*
> *– Maybe so, says Joe. They took the liberty of burying him*
> *this morning anyhow.*
> James Joyce, *Ulysses*

So I said to Jacoba
(Who they call Delene),
'Sissie, which is your
Real name?'

And Delene said,
'Reality? Johannes,
Look at your hands;
Imagine them dead
One day.'

12. THE END OF THE FIRST PERSON: AN INTRODUCTION

A hand cannot pray alone
Ingrid Jonker

Reconstructing the past ... becomes essentially an issue in the politics of the present. Making this move too quickly, however, risks effacing the 'historical' as a problematic almost entirely. It seems to me strategically – politically – necessary that we reclaim the historical in the face of such a fore grounding of the present, and the way in which this is best done is by reminding ourselves that, while we may acknowledge that the categories of the historical and the political are radically implicated, the acts of politicisation *and* historicisation *are not identical. To run them into each other is to avoid this central question: how can we make of history something both resistant to being simply appropriated by the present and yet relevant enough to relate meaningfully to the present?*

Michael Green, 'Re-thinking a Literature: Past
Significance and Present Meaning'

To paraphrase the poet,
History must resist the intelligence
Almost successfully.

In making you
(Johannes, Hester,
Jacoba, Johannes, Marianne)
I (peekaboo) make myself.

Against you,
The vanishing family,
I adopt my position.

No voice but mine
Echoing in what is only yours
Or not mine either.

I only see you
Through certain assumptions, yes,
But where you begin to blur
Interests me the most;

It is peripheral vision,
Not hindsight,
That makes the best history.

For if we *only talk about the past*
Mainly because we are interested in the present,
Then there is only the first person,
Lyrical Origin and End.

Cumulative indeed,
Constructed certainly, and
Socially shot through,
Position not essence, yes,

But simply a here and now,
Meaningless
Without a there and then . . .

You, the family Oosthuizen,
Are the other hand
Without which I Am
One clapping.

So here is *my* apology
(Sorry, Sir Sidney):
All this is only to speak again
Something disappearing

Into our severe disciplines,
To hear back from it
The echoes that make me
As I make them . . .

Because history (to cite again),
Is what hurts, resists,
Makes us
As we make it.

Let us, then, end today's lesson
By returning more directly to our text
From Mr Stevens:

Poetry
Must resist the intelligence
Almost successfully;

And you,
Marianne, Johannes, Jacoba,
Hester, Johannes,

Slipping out of sight,
Hold me in place
As I try to trace
Your swift descent

To me.

13. FROM STRUCTURE TO EVENT: WILLIE BRITZ

> *Take away from a painting all representation, signification,*
> *theme, text as intended meaning, take away also all the*
> *material (canvas, coloured paint) which for Kant cannot be*
> *beautiful in itself, rub out any drawing oriented toward a*
> *determinable end, take away its background and its social,*
> *historical, political, and economic support, and what is left?*
> *The frame, the framing, a play of forms and lines which are*
> *structurally homogeneous with the structure of the frame.*
> Jacques Derrida, 'The Parergon', 1979

It sounded like wagon wheels on a rough road
  approaching us through the darkness as they have
          across all our history.
I sleep badly, and was searching the house for a pill
          for my restlessness
When the sound made me draw my curtain,
  drew my eyes to the golden square
          of my neighbour's window;
There was Hettie, framed on the wall of the night,
          a portrait in terror,
Her mouth an O before the cry cut like a whip-lash
  across the gathering storm of hooves and rims
          closing in on her,
She running back and forth,
          appearing and disappearing
In and out of the limits that gave the shape and meaning
  to the frozen movement of her final moment.

Instinct had me sprinting for my door, but
                before I could pass through the frame
    I was stopped by a crack,
                a clap,
                        then a sough,
With Hettie's scream hanging high in the whispering air,
                left floating above
    her roof like paper folding and flaming,
                the crumpling shape her life had taken
Taking her and the invisible ones
                        stage-off
                she was screaming for
Down, down.

We would later praise her for saving us
                with her resonating fear
That woke us to flee before the stampede of beasts
    tugging
                the burdens of our past,
Those capsules in which we rode through time,
That century and a quarter
    alive now in the Preller-present, in which
His careful reconstructions
    have buried our straw hats and blesbuck-hide trousers
Under decent brocade waistcoats,
                spanking white kappies and aprons,
                        intricate tucks and delicate seams.

37

Our well-dressed sentries were posted to guard
    those ox-wagons,
                not us from them,
But the flickering frames of *De Voortrekkers*,
    of Blauwkrans, Moordespruit, Bloed Rivier,
Have drawn us in,
    outsiders made inner,
                to where they are still alive
                    and we, through *Volkskongres* and
                        Voortrekkermense alike,
    are directly in their path.

For what is a picture but its frame,
    and what are we
but those folding in on the spaces we've cleared,
                planes become depths,
    to swallow us,
        Gatvol.

14. FATHER LIKE WATER

(Oosthuizen, Johannes M.: 27.8.1927 – 3.8.1964)

> *. . . this is a speculation which presupposes the possibility*
> *that at an outer limit, the sense people have of themselves*
> *and their own moment of history may ultimately have*
> *nothing whatsoever to do with its reality . . .*
>> Fredric Jameson, 'Nostalgia for the Present'

They say that Shaka stopped here
On a raid down south
And asked for
Water
Where this river blurs
Into the sea;
Finding it sweet, he named the place
Amanzimtoti,
Pointing the way for servants of succeeding powers
To take their ease here.
And so we came from the high, dry land,
Our heady base for burrows that go below sea-level
To fuel our moment of supremacy,
To find again, like that king before us,
Our more private sustenance
Where earth and sea balance out.

My child, my eldest,
Had been ill, jaundiced

In the golden atmosphere we breathe all year,
But these three weeks of blues and greens
Have washed new colour over and into her;
From this I drink my deepest joy,
Tripled by the happiness of sister, brother, mother –
But today I must be Father,
Having given, knowing when to take,
Forcing the issue of our return.
Water wells at this,
Squeezes through lids,
Seeps from pools of perception
In which I define myself –
But there are other sources for my being,
Also concerned with controlling
Water.

My apprenticeship was served at Blyvooruitzicht as a
    plumber.
From there, I took my new family to Stilfontein, but the
    calm there
Turned stagnant, and seven years ago with a new-born
    son
I felt ready to return, to start again at my beginning.

The prospects are good for a man
Worried about water in this dry region;
Under its thirsty surface, hostile to farmers,
Water is the miner's real threat.
The first shaft sunk in 1910

Flooded and, despite imported steel casings,
Was abandoned to become a well
Serving a grateful but insignificant local community;
By 1934 our use of concrete began to work
Where the metal of foreign ingenuity
Had failed – around our new technology was built
The economy of a nation – and by the 1950s
The plumber had come into his own:
First eighty four megalitres per day we pumped,
Then one hundred and forty five,
So the gold could be raised
High and dry
Like a flag,
Purified
In the interests of our people,
Our once poor white people,
Now with prospects you could
(And the world did, despite
Sharpeville, saboteurs, and station bombs)
Bank upon.

Which meant, by 1964,
That I could use a new car's need of a service
As an excuse to cut short
Daughters, son, and wife
Crying for a longer drink
Of these sweet waters.
This was true, and logically irrefutable,
But still a cover for a need I could not explain

Or they understand –
The irrepressible tug towards the forty-nine week a year
Familiar, where my shape takes form,
Albeit mostly in complaints,
Where all the things I was taught and trained to be
(As opposed to those – like love and fatherhood –
Which are simply allowed to happen) find their sense;
Deeper than this even,
The pull of work as some kind of an answer
To questions which we do not even know how to pose,
Questions that may trouble one, nevertheless,
On a Monday morning, say,
At two twenty a.m . . .

The leave was owed me,
But who does not need to feel
Indispensable?
And water never sleeps.

. . . and what about the dog, I continued,
We can't expect Prinsloo
To feed it forever;
And the house?
Those cracks that scare you all,
The ceiling coming away from the walls,
The leaks that have stained our carpets,
Those pillars crumbling – we must get back to make sure
The Mine repairs our house or
Better still, moves us;

That's what you want, isn't it,
My Bokkie?

And how was I,
A plumber next to the sea, to know
That young Eugene MacMaster,
Playing in the street
Had seen a broken pipe,
And water disappearing down a new fissure in our
     garden;
Or that Prinsloo,
Faithful to more than his chore,
Had reported water bubbling out from the foundations
Of our home;

And how was I,
A plumber next to the sea, to know
How little the officials from the Mine knew
When they casually ordered the repair of these leakages,
Gave the all-clear,
And explained away our lives with the comment
That pipes often break
When the ground 'settles'?

How was anyone to know,
In 1964,
All the ways of this water we had fought and thought
We had mastered?
Certainly not a plumber with his family by the sea,

A king in his way in terms of
Race, class, and gender, who,
Like that king of this place in another time,
Lay lapped in water
While other waters, far less sweet,
Quietly ate away
The grounds of his existence.

15. VENTRILOQUIST WITHOUT A DUMMY: VOICES[1] FOR WORKERS

> *Goodbye the day, Good luck to me.*
> Inscription on Northumberland
> Miners' Safety Helmets

> *. . . the text is not a line of words releasing a single 'theological' meaning . . . but a multidimensional space in which a variety of writings, none of them original, blend and clash. The text is a tissue of quotations drawn from the innumerable centres of culture.*
> Roland Barthes, 'The Death of the Author'

Underground is never what you expected:
'Working in the grave is most uncomfortable.
You expect death to occur any time
In your daily work routine.' *We stand in lines,*
Thinking – how strange to be interred,
Open-eyed creatures buried alive!
'One does not feel hunger underground
Because of the anxiety to come out once more
To see the world again.'

'Before the great collapse I shall be home,'
But when I return there, clutching my bundle,
All I can find are shrivelled stalks
And empty huts; 'Home and his wife
Began to disappear into the distant past.

Sometimes he tried to figure out what his wife
Looked like: a picture of an odd, funny, dirty,
Unattractive woman came to his mind.
He could not think of desiring such a woman

For anything.' *Lesotho, now*
I leave you with your mountains . . .
I am going to the white man's place –
The tableland . . . 'Now I assume
Another blanket . . . In crossing the river
I become a new man, different from the one
I was at home. . . .' *We stand by watching the parades*
Walking the deserted halls, we who are locked
In the pits of gold. 'Roar and clang,'

You machines of the mines! 'In the dark tunnel
Of the mine . . . I become part of the machines,
A living ore-crusher . . . ' He putteth forth his hand
Upon the rock; he overturneth the mountains
By the roots. 'In the confines of that hole,
Men use great force to tear into the
Unyielding but not inert mass of rock.
They are not remote from the point of confrontation.
They are in it. Indeed, they are of it.'

The darkness stuns my normal senses. 'Attendants
At the feast glitter, wealth piles on the
Mountains.' *My brother also carries a pick.*
'We live in spans together'; *different*

Tribal groupings are unnoticeable
Below ground. 'Black miners in South
Africa "regard themselves as members
Of their work team first and foremost
And do not appear to have any interest in its

Ethnic composition."' *[Many] believe that God*
Does not pragmatically help them – He
Helps the whites only. 'I don't find hell
Would be like this': He setteth an end to darkness,
And searcheth out all perfection: the stones
Of darkness and the shadows of death.
'Down in our father's resting place
Where you, our ancestral spirits dwell,
They say': the thing
                    that is hid

Bringeth he forth to light.

1. The fabric of this text is woven from the following material: B.W. Vilakazi's
'Ezinkomponi' ('rendered into English verse' as 'The Gold Mines' by
Florence Louie Friedman); Dunbar Moodie's essay, 'Mine Culture and
Miners' Identity on the South African Gold Mines' (I have drawn especially
on the material he gathered from his 'informants' and 'participant observers'
– Aaron Mathabela, Sibysiso Mbatha, Henry Mothibe, Morris Tsebe);
Stephen Gray's 'Song of the Miners' from the 'Man's Gold' sequence; Mazisi
Kunene's 'The Gold-miners'; David Goldblatt's 'Shaftsinking' from *On the
Mines* by David Goldblatt and Nadine Gordimer; Job 28: 1-11 (authorised
King James Version). Of course, the ethic that demands *my* acknowledge-
ment of these sources reinserts the problem of agency into Barthes' thesis.

16. CALL ME DELENE

(Oosthuizen, Jacoba J.M.: 25.12.1951 – 3.8.1964)

> . . . *the years 1963-4 were those when the African*
> *Resistance Movement reached the peak of its activity, and*
> *when it was broken.*
> Stephen Clingman, *History from the Inside*

My grandmother's ghost lives
In my name – unspoken now,
My identity taking a more modern shape
That will age with the fashion of its time
More quickly even than did hers;
So the weight of the past lies buried
In the differences that we speak
Preserving its shape in
Silence
But still calling
Through contemporary tongues.

Ouma called me by her name:
Made me stay at table till
Cold vegetables congealed in glassy fat
Were consumed – this taking till
Four o'clock some dinner times.
Jaundice is easily diagnosed,
Cause for yellow envy in school friends
Wishing too for a quarter off – even

A holiday by the sea
(Geelsug kry seelug);
But all Papa's favouritism could not penetrate
The rejected plate,
Or the lonely communions
In the bathroom,
Where the toilet bowl was greedy for my secrets
And the mirror reflected the undisturbed bib
Of my gymslip;
Here was my realm
(Clinically diagnosed since 1873
But invisible in the Far West Transvaal
Of 1964 –
Except in the awkward grace
Of my pencil-stroke angles and lines):

Total control, Ouma Jacoba.

17.   JOHANNES'S LOVE SONG

Through metaphor to reconcile
the people and the stones
                    William Carlos Williams

My mind a deserted haulage
In the hours before blasting;
Your memory
Rests on a bench at a bullnose.

18a. TRANSLATION: *MISE-EN-ABYME*

> *Afrikaans is 'a personal, intimate language of the huge*
> *family-nation, and English is the hard commercial tongue*
> *of the world'.*
>> Gustav Preller, Letter to Nellie, 19/2/1919
>> (Thank you, Isabel)

Nothing set down here
Would have been
In English, of course;
And this act of recovery has been,
Perhaps, as futile
As any attempt to exhume
The Oosthuizens would have been –
For now they are buried again,
Lost, this time,
Not under the crumbling edges of the earth,
But in the vertigo
Of translation.

If, however, all history
Depends upon anachronism,
And to be *punished under a foreign*
Code of conscience is the condition
Of survival,
Then you must put up with strangers
Trying to find their way through

The twists and turns of your tongue,
Accept the phrase-book phraseology and guide-book
    garble
In which you now speak.

And as for those original documents,
Those signatures you scribbled in time
Not knowing they would become
The only clues to an afterlife,
Well, what did you leave us?

The words that live on beyond you, Hettie,
Written on holiday,
Arrived after you had returned home
Only to disappear
Far more permanently;
Between the posting and the delivery,
Your order to a newspaper
For a liquid carpet cleaner
On special offer
Took on the weight of all the earth
That covered you.
Here, to the letter,
Is how you ended
Your last letter:
'And I shall it value
If you the order
As quickly possible
To me will back send –

Because I it very need will
When I once back am.'

Well, it just shows
How wrong you can be,
And how badly heard
By posterity;
But what else can the future read
In its rough transliterations?

The only hope for all of us
Is that in tomorrow's reflections
Of what our yesterdays reflect,
We will see ourselves in the mirrors
Of two languages face to face
And bounce back and forth between them
Alive in an infinite series through time
Stretching to invisibility . . .

Because your dead-letter
Tells us so little;
Forgive us, then,
For looking for you and yours
In other places too;
It's just that we have to ask
What you would have written
Had you known there was just this
To come from where
You've gone –

Beyond correction,
Deletion, addition,
Beyond even the simple fact
Of no carpet, no floor, no foundation,
No ground – your last request:
Carpet cleaner.

And so . . .

18b. FREELY, FROM THE AFRIKAANS

. . . on to Pieter G. Mocke's poem. Published in Welkom in 1959, it is close enough in time and place to approximate an 'original' sense of our subjects – woolly caps pulled down tight to the eyes over the shaven heads of boys in short khaki pants and bare feet; the fat faces of little girls with unravelling cardigans stretched tight over cheap floral dresses; the collars of open-necked shirts peeping above the V-necked jerseys of jacketed men looking sternly out through their short-back-and-sides; the thoroughly-dated fifties frames of glasses magnifying the creases in the corners of the eyes of squinting mothers draped with their latest dirt-stained little ones; the Brylcreemed quiffs above the smooth, hard faces of seventeen year old fitters and turners turning the plaited heads of buck-like school girls . . . I want to think – with all the sentimentality that the working class invokes in the professional word-smith – that Mocke's collection, Die mes in my hand, Onbreekbare Huweliksband en Luilekkerland (The knife in my hand, Unbreakable Marriage Bond and Luxury Land), *is a more literal expression of white mine culture of the period – that the fact that it was published by 'My stokperdjie boekhandel en biblioteek' ('My Hobby[-horse] Book Dealers and Library') means that it is possible that here the amateur poet, by virtue of the very professional experience that makes him an amateur, has had the skill to catch the authentic voice of a brother plumber on the mines, now gone down his hole forever.*

'SKAGBODEM VAN DIE MYN EN 3.2 POMPSTASIE'
'SHAFT FLOOR OF THE MINE AND 3.2 PUMP STATION'

> *Just as, in the original, language and revelation are one
> without any tension, so the translation must be one with
> the original in the form of the interlinear version, in which
> literalness and freedom are united. For to some degree all
> great texts contain their potential translation between the
> lines; this is true to the highest degree of sacred writings.
> The interlinear version of the Scriptures is the prototype or
> ideal of all translation.*
> Walter Benjamin, 'The Task of the Translator'

3.3 Setlaars
3.3 Pioneers

Met geen gebroke been of vlerk
Firm in body and mind,
Doen elke Pompman skowwewerk;
Every pump man does his shift
Gewaarborg met 'n handelsmerk.
With the dedication that is his trade mark.
'n Skagvlak bo my hoof 3.3
A level above my head here in 3.3,
Is onbekend aan wie weet wie,
Unknown to anyone,
Die water styg soms tot die knie
The water rises to the knee

As daar van uit setlaarsgang
If a pipe coming out of the passage opened by pioneers
'n Pyp verstop en moeilikheid opdam
Is blocked and trouble builds up;
Is na herstellingswerk 'n elk nog moeg en tam.
Everyone is tired and weary after repair work,
Van daar daal neer na drie-drie damme
But water drops to the dams on three-three level,
Vloeiend water neer soos veldbrandvlamme:
Flowing like veld-fire flames
Waar naturel uit baie stamme
Where natives out of many tribes
Die meetstok in die water domp
Put the yardstick in the water
En water dophou wyl ons pomp.
And watch while we pump.
Vlytig, waaksaam, onverslap nooit lomp
Diligent, vigilant, unflagging, never clumsy,
Daar is 'n tydkaart opgestel
A time chart is established
Waarop die Ure's afgetel –
On which the hours are counted off –
Verdwyn die water op die spel
The water vanishes from the scene
As ons die pomp spoed neer moet vel!
As we increase the pump's speed!
Die bodem pompe pomp met spoed
The floor pumps pump furiously

Die damme word opnu hervoed –
And the dams are freshly filled
Want 5.3 vlak weer bo 3.3 geheel
Because, above 3.3, level 5.3 is repaired;
Laat waters meer industrieel
Let the water flow more industriously,
In 3.3 Setlaars voluit vloei;
Flat out in our stope
Sodat die tydkaart word geskroei –
So that we burn up the time chart
En oor die maat word deurgepomp
And everything over the measure is pumped through
Sodat die vloed die bodem nie oorromp.
And the flood does not overwhelm the floor.

II

In ons teenwordigheid
Our presence
Het ons verantwoordelikheid
Gives us responsibilities
In 'n groot sentrifikale pompgebied.
In a great centrifugal pump area,
Waar ordelikheid, geen slordigheid
Where things are orderly, and no messiness
En nimmer dom onnoselheid
And certainly never dumb stupidity
Of onkunde of skeltaal, swets
Or ignorance, cursing, swearing

Of vloek of skoor of helsgeklets
Profanity, squabbles, drivel from hell
Astrantheid nooit geskied.
And insolence ever happen.
Hier is ek basie, en hier is ek klasie
Here I am master, and here I am servant,
Hier op drie-drie en die bodem en 3.2 pompstasie
Here at the bottom on three-three and at 3.2 pump station
Geen renewasie en geen tormentasie
There is no renovation and annoyance;
Dog hier so val waarheid en grasie
Here truth and grace descend.
Skryf ek op 'n tafel in die groot pompkamer
I write on a table in the big pump room
Somtyds staande, dan sit ek waak oor alles.
Sometimes standing, or sitting and guarding everything.
En skryf toneeltjies, gedigte, resetasie,
I write scenes, poems, recitations,
So eg na talent vir ons Afrikaner nasie!
So true to the talent of our Afrikaner nation!
Tot iets moet gebeur met dramatiesie situasie.
Until something dramatic emerges from this situation.

Hier raak niks bekrompe
Here nothing becomes claustrophobic
Want ek let op na die Pompe.
Because I look after the Pumps.
Ek werk hier en waak, lees boeke van wraak;
I work here and watch, read books of revenge,

Van Liefdesromanse en speurverhale
Love romances and detective stories,
Vuurwarme Kultuur, Afrikaans bo alle andere tale!
Fiery Culture, Afrikaans above any other language!
So verhewe my siel vind nooit slytasie –
My soul is so exalted it never wears out –
Vir land en volk aldeur biografie.
My life given constantly for land and people.
Ek is die pompman vredevol vol harmonie:
I am the pump man, at peace and filled with harmony:
Pomp gedreun is 'n treffende Simfonie
The drone of the pump is a moving Symphony
Wat alles verkondig dat die lewensbestaan
That proclaims the existence of life;
Vir vroutjie en my word verniel nog verslaan.
*My good wife and myself are neither destroyed nor
  defeated*
Solank ek nie doen wat verbode is
As long as I don't do what is forbidden –
Doen ek tog wat verbied word met vrede en rus.
Yet I still do what is forbidden with peace and ease;
Laat die vlaters opstyg en voorwaarts vloei
Let those faults rise up and be washed away,
Ek bloei in my werk soos 'n Roosboom in bloei
I blossom in my work like a Rosetree in bloom
Om net te laat sien en streef op die baan
Just to be seen and strive on the way –
Ek is Pompman en elkeen moet weet ek bestaan.
I am a Pump Man and everyone must know that I exist.

Dis ek wat begeer – en dis God wat regeer
It is me that aspires – and it is God who governs
Om wat edel en rein is te versprei en beheer.
So that that which is noble and virtuous is spread and
controlled.
Ek gryp na die Kroon
I grasp for the Crown
Want dis heerlik om pompman te wees!
Because it is glorious to be a pump man!
Heerlik deur Rose en Dorings te vleg wie
Glorious to braid a wreath from Rose and Thorns for
those
Rus het in heilig gemoed
Who have the peace of a holy conscience
Waar die stroom van die lewe; aldeur vloeiend water my
In the stream of life – continually flowing water that
laaf en voed.
refreshes and feeds me.

19. THE BIG PICTURE

> *I said, 'Graham, what on earth do you think they'll call it*
> *in history?' and he said, 'I've just read a book that refers*
> *to ours as the Late Bourgeois World. How does that appeal*
> *to you?'*
>
> Nadine Gordimer, *The Late Bourgeois World*, 1966

The big picture,
So Dan will tell you,
Was the creation of a middle-class;
Nationalism, it seems,
For the Afrikaner,
Was *Ons Eerste Volksbank*,
Volkskas and *Uniewinkels*,
SANTAM and SANLAM – and, of course,
Federale Volksbeleggings,
Our way into the superstructures
Of mining.

For Johannes Oosthuizen,
It was the *Reddingsdaadbond*,
A trade, employment, insurance,
All woven into song and dance
In Afrikaans –
But you who have seen what the
Nationalists would give away:
The song, the dance, the pure white Afrikaans,

Leaving naked and stark
Property that's private,
Interests invested –
You can ask now,
What cost, a bourgeoisie?

Endless images
From forty lost years:
Lorries with domestic loads heading quite deliberately
        nowhere,
Workers less than the machines they operate,
Scattered bodies at odd angles in the dust,
Children's bellies pregnant with emptiness,
Bullets in a blackboard,
Screams echoing in clinical rooms . . .

. . . even a house,
An ordinary, middle-class house,
Disappearing down a hole . . .

Yes, you can ask now,
What cost, a bourgeoisie?

20. GRAVES: HETTIE'S EPIGRAPHY

O me, why have they not buried me deep
    enough?
Is it kind to have made me a grave so
    rough,
Me, that was never a quiet sleeper?
Maybe still I am but half-dead;
Then I cannot be wholly dumb;
I will cry to the steps above my head
And somebody, surely, some kind heart
    will come
To bury me, bury me
Deeper, ever so little deeper.
               Alfred Lord Tennyson, 'Maud; A Monodrama', II:xi

There is a small farm graveyard between the Vaal and the road to Venterskroon: barbed wire rotting in the tall, sharp grass still just demarcates one elongated, anonymous pile of stones and two marble-edged sites resisting with different degrees of firmness the neglect of families long gone – the farm, by the time of our visit to friends there for a picnic on their property, now piecemeal smallholdings beginning to be owned (as in the case of my ex-schoolmate who had married well) by commuters to Parys or Potchefstroom.

These graves we passed on our way to the river are nestled in a field where someone had just enough respect for the unknown dead to plough and plant around them, acknowledging their right to at least this much of the rocky plains, kloofs, and hills they appropriated and left as legacy to, as it now turns out, strangers.

One of the graves is called to our attention by our hosts, for its still proudly erect and well-carved headstone reads:

Vir God en Vaderland en Vryheid
For God and Fatherland and Freedom
Hier rus een
Here rests one
Bloedrivier held
Blood River hero
16 Des 1838
16 December 1838
P L J Van Vuuren
Met 4 eggenotes
With four wives
Geb 12 Maart 1812 – oorl 1889
Born 12 March 1812 – died 1889

Not just for God, Fatherland, and Freedom, hey, smiles my friend's husband, nudging mine; Blood River earned him four wives, too! Now, that's what I call a usable past!

I'll say this for Johannes; he bent over to the fallen stone of the other grave and asked, what's this? Together, he and I reconstructed the thin and weathered script:

In liefdevolle her-

In loving re-

in nering

mem brance

aan

of

Martha Jacomina

Maria Pretorius

Geb. Beljon

Born Beljon

Op 29 Sep. 1876

On 29 September 1876

Overl. 4 Des.

Passed away 4 December

1900 Gez 21:1

Nineteen hundred Psalm 21:1

Not one of the four, or even a fifth who survived him, then, but, then, who? No chance of heroism here, where a king's rejoicing in the victory God gives him becomes her epitaph; Van Vuuren has an identity attached to a date that gives a centre, a structure, to those of his birth and death: she, just the facts of her marriage, her twenty-four years, and the loving memories that probably killed her, in one way or another.

Now you have probably made more of this already than could I, a mother from the cover of *Die Huisgenoot* with whom your observations would be as out of place as that wristwatch Johannes laughed at on the arm of Joseph in last year's school Christmas pageant; in any event, our commemoration of the dead is nothing if not obvious in its reproduction of our prejudices. Still, it would have killed me then to know that the date on the stone that gives finished shape to my identity rounds off my family's too:

HIERDIE GEDENKTEKEN KYK UIT OOR
This Memorial Looks Out Over
DIE GEBIED WAAR DIE OOSTHUIZENGESIN
The Area Where The Oosthuizen Family
OP 3 AUGUSTUS 1964
On 3 August 1964
HULLE LEWENS GELAAT HET TYDENS
Lost Their Lives During
'N KATASTROFIESE GRONDINSAKKING
A Catastrophic Ground Subsidence

reads the plaque on our lump of granite.

And gazing out, as this inscription does from the flat face of our memorial perched on that protective arm above what is once again an almost empty tract, you can trace the grids of our ordinariness still: the roads ghost through, lines drawn from patch to patch of tar running out at the fences meant to keep you out; trees, *taller today*, the memories of our attempts to disguise the veld, are now flags that spell out our once private properties on The Property; foundations peek through where foundations were left, edging up to the circle of rubble jammed into the mouth that took roof, walls, floors, foundations and family too – a circle of silence filled with stone, difficult to swallow, even now.

There are all these clues, and more spectacular evidence besides: from all those front-page pictures and special edition colour-spreads that commemorate our loss you can re-create the layout of our community – not that this is necessary, of course, as it is reproduced all over the place in the proliferation of North, South, East, Westdenes that dot our maps where they are not too small for them. Of course, they no longer invoke those distant narrow wooded valleys we had never seen, but are simply words now through which we tried to establish a sense of direction in these landscapes we could not imagine, even, indigenously.

But tourism is for the living, and you must move along now, our site seen; leave our slab on this slope, where the view at night serves as a temptation for little daughters of the mine to come upon it for the first time, sandwiched between hot-pumping boys and our cold past; I'm too deep to care.

For you – Martha Jacomina Maria Pretorius *née* Beljon, and even you, P L J Van Vuuren, Blood River hero comfy in the bosoms of four wives – you were laid to rest by families who, if swallowed now by history, were left you long enough to bury you.

As for me and my house, family and all,

> 'GOD HET HULLE SELF TER AARDE BESTEL'
> *'God himself committed them to earth'*,

as our monument would have it. That God who so haunted me as a child that I would lie in bed afraid to hear my heart beat, in case I should hear it stop, and He would take me, another of His victories for which some king of some kind somewhere would thank Him. Yes, God buried us himself all right, in whatever shape he took that night – Economics, Geology, Politics; indifferent let us drop, and I put on no knowledge with his power in that trivial event; but like every mother I lie here now cradling my loss and shouting '*Give back my dead*!' And if those negative theologians are right and we can only know him apophatically, by what he is not, then we are the shape he takes today, the ghosts of his power, haunting your history.

21. APOPHRADES: OR, A BEGINNER'S MODERNISM

Uncoffined, unknelled, to his grave he was sped,
Unwept, with irreverent haste,
No requiem was sung, nor ritual read,
O'er his bed in the desolate waste –
His grave on the terrible waste.
A.G.E., 'The Digger's Grave on the Vaal'

24 October 1970
A sinkhole appeared on this Saturday afternoon at the
tennis courts of the miner's recreation centre at Venterspost,
swallowing part of the clubhouse and one spectator, Karl
Nortje. Four people [were] playing a game of tennis at the
time, and three others in the clubhouse ... narrowly
escaped ...

A.B.A. Brink, *Engineering Geology of Southern Africa*

I Karl Nortje,
Perceived the scene, and,
Not without some anxiety,
Foretold the rest –

It was in the October of 1970
That I, Karl Nortje,
Was sitting as reported
One quiet Saturday afternoon
In the clubhouse of the Venterspost
Miners' recreation centre
Having, as cliché will have it

And Professor Brink omits to mention,
A last brandy and coke
While watching four friends
At a game of tennis.

There were four of us spectators too,
Three of whom, as Brink says, narrowly escaped –
I was number four;
Along with a good proportion of the clubhouse,
I was swallowed whole
By that sinkhole –
And I'm prepared to admit
What the good academic's style forbids him,
That there is something quite amusing
About my exit,
Like falling off a chair in public –
Only in this case I wasn't able to get up,
Red-faced, dust myself off
And hide my embarrassment with that old standby,
'And now for my next act . . .'

After all,
How did Lazarus
Top his?

Still, it turns out that in this version
I've been given another trick up my sleeve
(A reward, perhaps, for bringing
The house down);

So, here I am again –
But, please remember that the circumstances
Which bring me to your attention here
Rather restrict me to
One-liners.

Oh, I know we're a comical bunch,
The whole lot of us, in our way –
Fall-down if not stand-up comedians:
The mine doctors tell stories
About our legendary drinking, for example;
You must have heard
The one about imposing a half-jack
On the x-ray of Visagie's liver,
Or the time when Van Es's wife put
Oil and Dettol in his bath when he was drunk,
And samboked him while he skidded about helplessly
On the enamel.

But surface clowns
Can be heroes underground:
You should have seen the likes of us
Take on the three hundred and sixty
Megalitres a day
That poured into a stope at West Driefontein
In 'sixty-eight;
Even old Brink
Cracked the clinical pose
Of his textbook prose

In his account of this:
'After an epic battle had been waged
Against the torrent for 23 days,
Two concrete plugs were successfully installed . . . ',
He almost enthuses
Before going on to report,
Straight-faced, matter-of-fact,
How the water
Got us back:

Caught us unaware,
Tracked us down
Even in our leisure time –
Six months after
My spectacular exit
At the tennis court,
The bowling green sank at
Venterspost recreation centre.
From the air
It could be seen that
This hole lined up with
The one from which I speak to you
And two earlier ones,
Innocent in the veld,
But silently,
Inevitably,
Closing in
On us.

It took a while,
But by 1975 we had learnt to avoid,
If not entirely control,
These unfortunate byproducts
Of our means of production –

they happen harmlessly now: sudden subsidences
somewhere out in the sleeping veld, sensed just ahead of
time by a meerkat, perhaps, sprinting away over the
sparse, dewy grass

– just in time, of course,
For other sorts of underground problems
To surface;
But with this the allegory
Becomes rather heavy-handed,
Despite all the attempts
Of our infamous social engineering
To keep the obvious at bay.
Still, let's let it, at last,
Come thumping home:
Pumping as hard as we could,
We could not stem the flow
Of Durban 'seventy-three,
Luanda 'seventy-four,
Soweto 'seventy-six . . .

It seems I shall die at the beginning of an era;
When history is against you,
A common refuge is metaphysics;

Given my present condition,
Who in this story
Is better qualified to make
Such an appeal?
So, if God is the last laugh
Somewhere beyond our punch-lines,
I join him now
With my mouth full of sand
And, from the omniscience of my extinction,
What I see,
With Blyvoor behind me,
Is the end of our history –
That history that so many saw as the
'Concentration of world history'
In which we modern Manichees lived out
Racism's Last Word –
For the contraries of our obsessions
Dissolve now,
Diluted into the hum-drum of democracy,
The day-to-day of civil liberties,
The various and dubious freedoms
That sweep us away now
As we emerge from our past,
Fall into your present,
Disappear into another's future.

No apocalypse,
No whimper even –
No, for I, Karl Nortje,

Mere spectator,
It's just a game of tennis,
An afternoon drink in the clubhouse
And then
No more of me;

I join the Oosthuizen family,
The West Driefontein morning shift,
And a gathering host of once-scattered
Others swelling into
Communities, villages, cities,
A nation, even,
Pouring out of a broken pipe
Into a hole in history;
I flow into all these others
Until otherness itself
Lacks its necessary reference
And we blur into everything
And nothing,
Awaiting you . . .

So I, Karl Nortje,
Perceived the scene and
Foretold the rest:
Looking happily forward,
I raised my glass, and,
Lips parted in anticipation,

Sank,
Without trace

(The good tidings which the historian of the past
brings with throbbing heart
may be lost in a void the very moment
he opens his mouth)

THE END

SECTION 2: MEDIATION

APPENDICES

APPENDIX 1:

MARGINALIA

1. THE ART OF POETRY

A poem must mean
To be.
(not quite) after Archibald MacLeish

In art there are
No accidents,
She said;
The smallest detail
Has to mean something.

All the while
Her eye was following
Him as he walked away;
Now there's an arse poetica,
She said.

2. FAILURES WITH METAPHOR

> *. . . truths are illusions of which one has forgotten that this is what they are; metaphors which have become worn out and have lost their sensual power.*
>> Friedrich Nietzsche, *Ecce Homo: How One Becomes What One Is*

TAKE 1: 1972

My mind is like a midnight subway;
Your memory is the tramp
Sleeping in the corner.

TAKE 2: 1979

My mind a subway
At midnight;
The memory of you
Sleeps in the corner.

TAKE 3: 1993

Mind a subway at midnight;
Memory sleeps in the corner.

3.   A MATERIALIST AESTHETICS

The faces of the poor
Are more interesting
Than those of the rich;
Which tells us
Nothing,
Except that poverty
Is a fine sculptor.

4. ETHICS

> *But they would forgive him; for he would tell them a story.*
>   Virginia Woolf, *The Waves*

If I could turn all this
Into poetry,
Would they forgive me?

  – for getting it all wrong:
the subject, the characters, the issues;
the wrong class, the wrong race . . .
given this time and place –

If I could turn this all
Into poetry,
Would you forgive me?

  – for the time it took away from you
to write it, and all the rest, *what
And how much you know* –

If I could turn even this
Concern with poetry and forgiveness
Into poetry,
    Should
  Anyone
        Forgive me?

> *Among the tortures and devastations of life is this then –*
> *our friends are not able to finish their stories.*
>   Virginia Woolf, *The Waves*

5. AUTOBIOGRAPHY

. . . die pateties-menslike verhale daaragter . . .
From the *Naweek-Vaderland* report on the
Blyvooruitzicht Disaster, 8 August, 1964

No pine trees grow in Pinetown,
A town named after Benjamin Pine;
And though I pine for Pinetown,
My hometown is no town of mine.

6. FOURTH OF AUGUST, 1994

Thirty years to the day
Yesterday
And the earnest historian

Missed it.

APPENDIX 2:

SOURCES

EXTRACTS FROM 'TOWARDS A NOTE ON THE SOURCES OF *SINKING*'

by Donnée Phelps

(*In Memoriam*)

The epigraphs in *Sinking* take on a variety of relations to the poems they head, but generally speaking they act in much the same way as the inscriptions on gravestones – fragments that are meant to capture whole lives (works), surface signals of buried histories. Within the grammar of our culture, these are the dots that signify ellipses.

....

Cawood Green seems to have studied many contemporary accounts of the Blyvooruitzicht incident. The various spellings of the mine's name that occur in the poem are all to be found in different versions of the incident – evidence that the very signifier of this disaster was extremely unstable at the time, and an indication of the as yet not fully-formalised nature of the language in which it chiefly happened. Linguistics and geology share hidden insecurities, are equally precarious as disciplines, and have the same potential for swallowing whole a variety of events.

Many of the sections of the poem take their controlling metaphor from newspaper reports, usually from eye-witness accounts. For example, John Coetzee (the names used are authentic) told Joe Loretz of the *Landstem* that, when awakened by the first rumble, 'sy eerste gedagte was dat diewe besig is om (in) te breek' and that 'hy het sy rewolwer – wat hy altyd byderhand in die slaapkamer hou – gegryp en buite gestorm'; he is quoted in the report as saying, '"Toe ek in die rigting van die Oosthuizen-gesin se huis kyk was daar niks. Net 'n stofwolk was in die straatlig sigbaar . . .'".

Again, details in the Willie Britz poem are taken from the *Carletonville Herald*: 'Teen ongeveer twee-uur Sondagnag was 'n buurman van die Oosthuizens, mnr. Britz, besig om 'n pil te soek vir sy rusteloosheid toe hy 'n geruising buite gehoor het wat vir hom geklink het soos wawiele op 'n ruwe pad'; what could be taken as a rather forced association of the coming disaster with an image straight from the heart of Afrikaner historico-mythology turns out to be a detail produced from the horse's mouth, as it were.

....

Sinking is, of course, saturated with poetic allusions. It is almost as if Cawood Green, whose critical work to date has focused on the novel form, felt he had to display his credentials in the field of poetry. Poetry is a form of writing he is known to dislike, primarily because of its association with the indulgent expression of personal emotion. 'The Death of the First Person: An Introduction', in which Cawood Green briefly and hesitatingly shows his decidedly unmanicured hand, is a clear statement on this, although early drafts of this section are even more overt. 'Death' was originally entitled 'The Trap of the Lyrical', and one version includes a defensively dismissive parenthesis that reads:

Poetry
(Always accepting
Nothing so prissily precious
Preserves itself here)
Must resist the intelligence
Almost successfully

The 'here' here is probably a reference to the troubled place of 'high' poetry in the South African situation, especially in the anti-apartheid period, but Cawood Green's own general ambivalence regarding his medium still comes through.

References to canonised high modernists abound, although this seems to have been part of a programme Cawood Green used to distance himself from the sort of projects with which he knew his poem would attract – certainly negative – comparisons. The reference in 'A Washing Machine at the End of the World' to Ezra Pound and Vivien Eliot's annotations on *The Wasteland* (taken from the '*Facsimile and Transcript of the Original Drafts*') suggests a desire on Cawood Green's part to step right through the looking-glass of that poem into the domestic world of its generation and production. The obvious parodic elements (Karl Nortje/Tiresias in 'Apophrades') speak for themselves and are generally associated with Eliot. Auden appears often, but seems to be taken more at face value. The embedding of lines from 'In Praise of Limestone' in various sections of *Sinking* (one even emerges in the marginalia – see 'Ethics') is apt not only for the way in which this poem sets up the extended geological metaphor, but also for the arbitrary connection of the date of its composition with the victory of the National Party at the polls in South Africa (a connection established in 'Older Than Time'). Other 'buried' allusions to Auden may be found in other poems ('Translation', 'Graves'). Yeats of course features in the concluding passage of 'Hettie's Epigraphy'.

....

The allusions to a history of Southern African poetry are not always as easy to spot or account for. When used as epigraphs, the references are acknowledged and can be looked up in most of the better anthologies of Southern African poetry now being produced. Hidden, or partially acknowledged allusions (italics, quotations) – like those to F.D. Sinclair's 'Free State' in 'Older Than Time', Schreiner's 'The Cry of South Africa' in 'Graves: Hettie's Epigraphy', Kunene's *Emperor Shaka the Great* in 'Apophrades', and Ruth Miller's 'Submarine' and Anthony Delius's 'Lady Anne Bathing' (ironic counterpoint to the epigraph for 'A Washing Machine at the End of the World') in 'Falling (Hettie's Love Song)' – appear to be part of an attempt to give the poem a little of the strength of its national heritage. There is, after all, in the very title of the final poem ('Apophrades' – the return of the dead) a possible reference to Harold Bloom's *The Anxiety of Influence* (1973).

The poem most dependent upon other poetic sources is, of course, 'Ventriloquist Without a Dummy: Voices for Workers' – while the footnote acknowledges the poems used here, it is worth noting that this does not account for all the ways in which 'Ventriloquist' is structured; the form of the stanzas, for example, is borrowed from Vilakazi's nine-line stanzas in 'The Gold Mines', suggesting a deeper structural debt to this poem than to the others that are pillaged for 'Ventriloquist'.

....

References to other sorts of texts also abound. 'Dan', in 'The Big Picture', is Dan O'Meara, the South African historian now resident in Canada and well known for his *Volkskapitalisme: Class, Capital and Ideology in the Develop-*

ment of Afrikaner Nationalism 1934-1948 (1983) (the thesis of which the poem approximates – although this will be clearer in O'Meara's forthcoming *Forty Lost Years*). There is a wide range of reference to various works of history – usually with a historiographical emphasis – from Ginzburg's wonderful book onwards, which I am not competent to trace. Many of these, however, are openly acknowledged in the epigraphs. The 'Isabel' of the epigraph to 'Translation' must be Isabel Hofmeyr, for whose work Cawood Green has professed immense admiration. The Michael Green of 'Re-thinking a Literature: Past Significance and Present Meaning' is, as far as I can establish, no relation to Cawood Green.

....

APPENDIX 3:

DEFINITIONS

SOME WORKING DEFINITIONS

History is history and it should remain so.
Dr Hendrik Verwoerd, Durban, 26 August 1963

1. 'HISTORY':

To articulate the past historically does not mean to recognise it 'the way it really was'. It means to seize hold of a memory as it flashes up at a moment of danger.
Walter Benjamin, 'Theses on the Philosophy of History'

2. 'ROMANCE':

The point of view in which this tale comes under the Romantic definition lies in the attempt to connect a bygone time with the very present that is flitting away from us.
Nathaniel Hawthorne, Preface to *The House of the Seven Gables*

3. 'ALLEGORY':

This people, plunged wholly in the present, lives with neither myths nor consolation.
Albert Camus

4. 'PROPHECY':

For the gods perceive things in the future, ordinary people things in the present, but the wise perceive things about to happen.
Philostratus, *Life of Apollonios of Tyana*

5. 'SURVEY':

The successful engineer of the future should know, not only how to locate his work, but how to locate it so that Nature will aid him in its building and take it under her protection.
    Professor John C. Branner of Stanford University, in a paper delivered in New York to the American Society of Civil Engineers, 1897

6. 'DOMESTIC DRAMA':

Family Reconstitution. A method developed by Louis Henry and used in HISTORICAL DEMOGRAPHY. Like genealogy, it consists of collecting information about the births, marriages, and deaths of all known members of a given family. Unlike the genealogist, the demographer reconstitutes families not for their own sake but as samples . . .
    Alan Bullock and Oliver Stallybrass (eds), *The Fontana Dictionary of Modern Thought*

7. 'AND NONE OF THE ABOVE':

About twenty kilometres from Dordrecht, a rough dirt road negotiates a minor ridge through a pass called Pappasnek. This is in the Swempoort area, and it is perhaps worth mentioning that Swempoort is miles from anything in which it is possible to swim, or any pass other than Pappasnek; the area was named after a trading store which used to be situated at another distant pass near a swimming hole, but was relocated to this slightly more accessible trading position during hard times. The store has since ceased to exist entirely. It was while passing through this trace of a place that I was told, by a local farmer, how Pappasnek came to be so named.

It seems that one of the white pioneers in this region was plagued by lions attacking his stock. He organised his sons into a hunting party, which he led, and soon enough the lion in question was located, shot – but only wounded – and disappeared into some long grass nestled into the ridge in question. The father ordered his sons into the grass to finish the lion off, and when they refused this dangerous command, stormed in – only to have the lion launch itself onto him and drag him to the ground. The eldest son showed admirable self-possession under the circumstances; he moved in, and squeezed off a shot that missed the father by a whisker (literally) but killed the lion. The beast was pulled off, whereupon the quite badly mauled father leapt up and tried to shoot his sons for cowardice. It took all four of them to restrain him, despite his wounds. He was dragged back to his farm, kicking, biting, and swearing, and the gap in the ridge near where this incident took place is called Pappasnek to this day.

The point of this story (CHOOSE ONE) is:

1. Historical significance derives from the material circumstances that determine it – in this case, the means of production that made it necessary to kill the lion, and the relations of production that gave rise to the patriarchal system that structured the event.

2. There is only a point to such a tale if we are able to 'claim a certain latitude' from the 'very minute fidelity' a *historical* version would demand. Names and places can be changed to protect the innocent.

3. The father stands for P.W. Botha, the lion for apartheid

South Africa, and the sons for F.W. de Klerk, Nelson Mandela, Mangosuthu Buthelezi, and a visiting nephew by marriage of a local resident who happened to be passing through. Shifting signifiers, as !Khoisan X/Benny Alexander has realised, are of extreme significance for the content of a story.

4. Near Pappasnek there are a number of small caves. In these it is still possible to find the skeletons of poaching Bushmen and recalcitrant black labourers who fell victim to the ideas of justice enforced by the farmers of this area. These bones, omitted from the anecdote, will rise again and reclaim their land – and this story. In their writing, South African historians all too often *resemble M. Terentius Varro, 'most learned of all the Romans', who 'is supposed to have forgotten the future tense in the first version of his Latin grammar'*.

5. Both Swempoort and Pappasnek are too small to feature on any map.

6. a) A lonely lioness is a very sad thing.

   b) The domestic and the aesthetic are inimical, viz. Olive Schreiner:

   You remember that long ago I told you how, nearly twenty years ago, when I was at Dordrecht, I had such a horror of eating before people, I couldn't, and how I used to have to eat alone, and how it kept on all the time my periods stayed away, and I told you what unkind, untrue things they said about it . . . Harry, the world isn't fair, I haven't sinned so much more than other people to be hunted down so.

   > Letter to Havelock Ellis, 1889. (Cronwright-Schreiner omitted 'all the time my periods stayed away' from his 1924 collection of her letters.)

Schreiner probably lost her virginity in Dordrecht, certainly had a pregnancy scare, and nearly married Julius Gau, the man involved. As it was, instead of a family, she produced *Undine* out of her time in the thickets of the region.

c) All of the above (1–6), as shared around the dinner table the evening after the incident.

APPENDIX 4:

COMMENTARY

AUTOLYCUSTHONY AND THE BLACK HOLE:

Cawood Green's *Sinking* as 'None of the Above'

by Alan Murray Charles

In so far as Autolycus is a thief, a pickpocket, and a cheat, he could, in the study, be unpleasant. But his crimes are understandable, and in a sense, even healthy, and, felony or not, they are venial in comparison with those of Leontes. On the stage the crimes of Autolycus are hardly felony at all; they are primarily tricks . . .

    J.H.P. Pafford, Introduction to the Arden Edition of *The Winter's Tale*, London: Methuen, 1963, p. lxxx

'A snapper-up of unconsidered trifles . . . '; from its subject to its method, *Sinking* follows the practice of Autolycus, with Cawood Green playing the tinker of historiography and the petty thief of poetry. The Blyvooruitzicht incident seems randomly selected, almost incidental to the greater narrative of the history with which the poem is concerned. Equally, the compendium of references littered about this subject – epigraphs, quotations and allusions (hidden and pronounced), parodies, translations, transliterations, inscriptions – almost becomes the subject of the poem as it defies any organising principle other than the attraction the references present for the writer.

    The various parts of *Sinking* are always something more than their sum, and the role of Cawood Green in their production follows the significance, as plotted by Pafford, Autolycus has for the action of *The Winter's Tale*:

Earlier he is so central that it can almost be said – as surely he would have said – that it is he, Autolycus, who is compassing the motion of the play, so to speak: later, as events change, he becomes merely one of the puppets and a minor puppet, and he senses the change.

The collector becomes collected, then, the ventriloquist (to borrow from the title of one of *Sinking's* more obviously 'stolen' sequences) spoken by his dummy. Any more inflated sense of the construction of *Sinking* would be to misinterpret the mode of the poem. Cawood Green parodies the potential categories to which it could be consigned on his title page; the 'history' with which the poem is concerned certainly makes more sense when read as 'romance', but, once opened up to other generic options, it becomes all too easy to read it as a rather one-dimensional 'allegory' or (and the overt anachronism of its representation makes this invitation very tempting) 'prophecy' for events since come to pass. These alternatives are so obvious as to be dismissible and the continuing list – 'survey' (a reference to the geological material, no doubt) and 'domestic drama' (Cawood Green's own marriage is known to have been a stormy one) – extends the question of the poem's generic status to the ludicrous. It is finally as 'none of the above' that *Sinking* must be considered.

The issue of classification raises itself in a more pertinent way when one comes to placing the poem in terms of period/ style. *Sinking* is a tempting target in so far as it may come across as a more-than-belated and cliché-ridden attempt to produce a South African *Wasteland*; indeed, Stephen Holmes takes just this stance in his famous review of the poem:

Let me start by saying that Cawood Green writes the sort of poetry that made me give up writing poetry. Not content with aspiring to a *Wasteland* for South Africa, he launches this plastic dinosaur as if the Jurassic age were still upon us. Modesty, too, he lacks: he attempts not only to join but subsume a tradition without an iota of the individual talent either of these tasks would require, even if they were to the point.

It is precisely the reading of *Sinking* as an approximation of a high modernist project that leads to this kind of assessment. (Phelps, in her path-breaking – if at times inaccurate – but tragically incomplete 'Note' on the sources of the poem, was amongst the first to warn against such metropolitan domestications of Cawood Green's work.) The poem in fact declares its distance from modernism in its reflexive avoidance of the gathering coherence usually to be found poised behind modernism's characteristic surface fragmentation. Things fall apart in the modernist project only to reveal the logic of a new system, an authority that develops in its apparent absence, whereas *Sinking* flaunts its all too obvious analogical significance in order to indicate that this ordering device exists in what is at best an incidental relation to the more important localised effect of the poem's details.

Much the same can be said for *Sinking*'s narrative structure. Focused as it is on 'a *moment* of danger', the poem does not represent the Blyvoor incident as an 'event', in either narratological or historiographical terms. If, as the narratologists say, an event is defined as 'the transition from one state to another state', the sinkhole disaster does not qualify as a story: it signifies the collapse of a sequence, the implosion of a development – in short, an end. In historiographical terms, too, it is concerned with an 'end' rather than continuing causal links – more specifically, it takes as subject the 'end of history' altogether, at least Southern African history. Apartheid is so implicit to the representation of the region and its periodisation, governing these in the way even its most vehement opponents are constructed in relation to itself, that attempts to nullify it leap beyond not just an *anti*-apartheid position, but even a *post*-apartheid position. The latter is as caught within the grammar of the structures it challenges as the former, for its 'new' position can still only be defined in relation to what it replaces.

Sinking, a poem concerned with the erasure of apartheid, is set in the middle of the dominance of grand apartheid because it is interested in exploring the failure of apartheid to achieve being at all; this attitude must not only infiltrate the period of the implementation of such a policy, but even *pre*-date the very conception of apartheid if we are truly going to get beyond it. Apartheid can only be transcended if it never existed. Granting it existence traps us forever in 'anti-s' and 'posts' to the degree that we must *always* be defined by it. No transition is free from the place it began. No destination is a complete break from its point of departure. Nothing is entirely new if it remains connected to the place it left by the process of transition.

It is in this sense that all Autolycusthony, the sleights of hand that lead to acquisition, would only be felonious if they were meant to contribute directly towards a structure, rather than being the tricks which, by virtue of their own lack of seriousness and substance, reveal the emptiness that not even structure can shape. The end of the poem is not accidentally marked by Walter Benjamin, and *Sinking* moves deliberately towards the 'void' Benjamin predicts. What

Hannah Arendt says of Benjamin's 'basic approach' is a clue to *Sinking*'s very lack of project; its aim is

> not to investigate the utilitarian or communicative functions of linguistic creations, but to understand them in their crystallised and thus ultimately fragmentary form as intentionless and non-communicative utterances. ... What else does this mean than that he understood language as an essentially poetic phenomenon?

We must qualify the grandeur of this prose when applying it to Cawood Green, of course, and we can do this by reminding ourselves that, while Shakespeare's Autolycus sings, he speaks entirely in prose. And, while Cawood Green may deeply concern himself with other people's 'unconsidered trifles', as the agent behind *Sinking*, he drops his ill-gotten gains, one by glittering one, into the blackest of holes. Each of Cawood Green's creations follows a vertiginous path into a gravitational pit in the flexible mat of space and time so deep that none of their light, let alone matter, can ever climb out. Having shifted to this metaphor (one that in true modernist form takes us, like the poem, from the particular to the universal – and then on into postmodern hyperspace), we must remember that black holes are not just bottomless space-time pits; they have, according to their most advanced theorists, personalities:

> the horizon of the big hole should pulsate in and out, ... and those pulsations should produce gravitational waves – ripples in the curvature of space-time that propagate out through the Universe, carrying a symphonic description of the hole,

writes Kip Thorne. Apartheid, crashing through the very fabric of our reason, has sent out just such waves, and swallowed more pain than its symphony can sing; there can be no truer way to celebrate its end than to prove that, like the theory of black holes, it existed only in its effects – and that the logic it would take to understand it will take us through a worm-hole to a new universe where it never existed.

Sinking is an exercise in just such a logic. As far as the past is concerned, it is an attempt to cross the 'event horizon' and enter a historical non-space 'older than time'. Its prophetic element is limited to the experience of the future we are told would accompany the entering of a black hole – that is, a vision of all that is to come, but rushing by in a way that would preclude any sort of analysis – thus serving mainly as an introduction to annihilation *magic is afoot,* 'the sky, earth, sea, air, abyss, and hell, all is God' . . . *I don't think I was particularly brave, but I couldn't bear the thought of Sherry* [Carol Sabatina's cat – ed.] *disappearing into the hole. So I just went back into the house to fetch him* . . . denies the materiality of apartheid, its economic determinants . . . *concentrate* . . . an insult to the real suffering of those his poem ignores . . . generic instability/ghost history . . . *time becomes no longer a construct whereby events can be structured and chronologically sequenced, but rather a concept which effects the interpretation of events* . . . Verwoerd was trying to read a question put to him through P.W. Botha's glasses (he'd left his in his office) when he was assassinated in the House of Assembly . . . spectacles/ordinary – *time it was and what a time it was, it was* . . . touts sold tickets for the first battle of Bull Run . . . *But shall I mourn for that, my dear? . . .'* in a few cases, local geology

has not been favourable nor was it studied
      in advance with resulting difficulties
           during construction and,
               occasionally,
                    actual failures.
Constructive study of failures is always useful . . .'
Yes, given what we knew,
      Anyone would have built a house here,
   Laid out a village even,
     Moved his love,
           Never suspecting.

His was always a story with a hole in it.
J.M. Coetzee, *The Life & Times of Michael K.*

SECTION 3: PRESENT

AFTERWORD

AFTERWORD: THE SECRET HISTORY OF *SINKING*

by Michael Green

The question which initiates a history is neither simple or given.
  Pierre Macherey, *A Theory of Literary Production*

This is a story by Michael Cawood Green. I first met him
when he was singing under his real name at a local club.
He was performing, solo with a guitar, a song of his own
entitled, 'If You've Got a Good Chord Why Change It'. At
least, I assumed that was what it was called, because the
chorus consisted of the repetition of that line until the
audience squirmed.

*

To be quite honest, my mind wasn't really on anybody's
performance that night; I'd had a bad start to the evening.
I hadn't planned to go out, was in fact trying to phone my,
as they say, 'estranged' wife, when what I heard on the line
was:
  'You have reached 456292 . . .'
  Confronted by this combination of two of the more
irritating features of the telephone, answering machines and
wrong numbers, I was about to hang up – but such simple
mistakes never let you off lightly; my hand froze a moment
too long to my ear as I hesitated between subjecting my
accidental contact to a murmured apologetic message or
one of those irritatingly enigmatic dead-letters of the phone-
age, and before I realised it I was being drawn into the rest

of the message:

'. . . I am unable to come to the phone right now. It is six twenty in the afternoon, and I'm about to climb into a warm bath with a glass of red wine. I have taken 150 Tuinals, and expect to be dead within a few hours. If you care enough, you can intervene – if life is such a matter of chance, I don't see why death shouldn't be – although those who know me well will understand what I'm doing. Just please don't try and save me at the cost of my having to live with some sort of irreparable physical or mental damage. That really wouldn't solve any of my problems, would it? So, note the time, and don't expect me to return your call. Over to you. 'Bye.'

Well, no question there – I swung into action; time? – just past eight . . . I'd no idea as to the effectivity of Tuinals, but my conscience took precedence over the status of this unknown party's quality of life. It's rare to be given a course of action so direct, so clear – grab the phone book, find the trauma unit number of the local hospital – much fumbling, book dropped, place lost – start again while mumbling into the mouthpiece, 'Uh, hold on, I'll, um, hang on . . . ' – found, I jammed down the receiver, and began to dial . . .

It hit me then, of course. In a panic I slammed the receiver into the cradle again and jabbed at the redial button – only to hear the clear numerical clicks signalling half a trauma unit number. All that lost voice was to me now was a wrong number, a wrong number I had just erased beyond recall. I contacted the police, but this was simply an embarrassing exercise. I reported that somewhere in the greater metropolitan area there was a woman attempting suicide, cynical enough at the last to indulge in a little answering-machine roulette. The constable on duty explained to me the primitive nature of our local telephone record service (detailed billing was not yet in effect on my six-digit number) and the mathematics of the variables involved; took my name and number, said, unenthusiastically, that he'd see what he could do.

I don't know what this says about my moral sensibility, but the whole episode was made even more upsetting for me because she had sounded attractive: well-spoken, confident, a touch of humour in the voice of someone clearly pretty, companionable, desirable – and by now probably dead in a cooled bath with a swirl of red wine drifting up from the drowned glass.

Enough decisive action for one day.

*

The call to my ex-wife now seemed rather redundant – I'd also had enough humiliation for one night – and the silent presence of the telephone was now so oppressive that I wandered out to a nearby club I frequented – and walked into the intriguingly unpopular display of 'If you've got a good chord why change it'.

The verses of this song weren't much relief for the at best bemused audience; one verse, if memory serves, went something like:

> A centre-fold splattered with semen,
> That's not art – that's a fact;
> And when it comes to craftsmanship
> I can do better with one hand tied behind my back.

This was followed by a number of other 'If you've got a good chord why change its . . . ', and then that single chord ground slower and slower until it almost stalled on a painfully-paced:

If you've got a good chord why change it
Let the tension build
Until it creates a resistance
And the whole fucking thing just folds . . .

At which point the song more or less ran out, rather than ending.

There was a little scattered applause, and certainly no call for an encore, as Cawood Green – who'd had his eyes closed tight during the whole performance – left the stage and blurred into the shapelessness of the evening. Later however, at the bar, I found myself squeezed next to him. I was in no mood for any more of the kind of posturing I'd more or less written him off to, but when we emerged from the counter crush I was faintly surprised to see that he'd shrunk into himself; he was smaller than he'd appeared on stage, and seemed to be trying to make himself even smaller (he was verging on the unforgivable for an artist, that is, being slightly overweight). After his nervy prowling around the small performance area – which, when he wasn't locked into place by the necessity of the microphone, it looked as if he was trying to explore or escape – he now looked deflated, directionless, free of image to the point of disappearance.

The space available to us was limited; retreat from the bar led to a confrontation with a litter of tables fully stocked by people who had people to talk to, and loners lounged in every vague access route. The pressure to make a comment of some kind built until I tried to defuse it with:

'What chord was that?'

'E minor,' he replied, slightly taken aback and clearly not having expected me to address him. More embarrassed silence followed.

'They're all so dismissive here of the three-chord trick,' he suddenly blurted, 'but the really skilled song-writers can get away with two, and the best, one; just watching someone ride the tension of pulling off a one-chord song generates a real suspense that invades every element of whatever else the song is trying to do. No place to hide there – you know what you're doing or you just go home.'

'Well, I must be off,' I said, registering as I said it that I didn't intend the impression my poor timing made inevitable.

*

It was just that my wrong number in her bath had floated back up to me, with the wine stain in the water now an effusion of red hair drifting around a pale face. If I wasn't careful she'd soon have flowers drifting from those hands cut off at the wrist by the water; Ophelia – naked now, of course, all goose bumps and hard nipples reaching away from a water line embracing curves, drifting into hollows, flooding groves of wet uncertainty and investigating once-secret creases and folds . . .

*

Cheap, I know, but I've always been weakest at the visual arts, the result of exposing myself to art classes at high school; Mr Gebhardt had ensured my inability to continue creating in this sphere – while at the same moment inspiring my desire to study it – by holding up one of my works in class and saying, 'Let's see what message Mr Green has for the world today.' He had hit the nail right on the head, of course; even then, in Standard Eight, I'd been embarrassed by my almost uncontrollable tendency to turn anything I'd tried to create into a sermon. Sermons, of course, depend upon the sins that inspire them, and even now I haven't acquired enough theory (despite four years of tertiary History of Art) to distinguish between the pornographic and the erotic – as my failure to combat the increasingly insistent fantasies filling out that dead, disembodied voice must make all too obvious.

*

Come to think of it, though, my fantasies in this case were perhaps a little closer to the truth than that painting I was undressing: the background for *Ophelia*, after all – that effusion of closely observed nature – is an imported frame for Millais' actual subject; the river, reeds, moss, and flowers were painted in the summer of 1851 on the banks of the River Ewell in Surrey. 'Ophelia', that is, Elizabeth Siddal (or 'Guggums' as her then-lover, later unhappy husband and even later remorseful widower, Dante Rossetti, was alone allowed to call her), had to lie in a bath in London for four months through the winter of 1851-52 to earn her eternal fame as someone else. Sir John did warm the water with lamps, and defy my imagination by draping her in an antique gown, but this first of the 'stunners', as the Pre-Raphaelites called the beautiful women they collected, had as little chance of surviving her association with great art as anyone else immortalised by it. Ruskin, infatuated, may have encouraged Lizzie in her desire to draw and write 'verses', but none of her pictures or poems survive, and the exercise was not enough to prevent her from taking an overdose of laudanum while the possessive and suspicious Rossetti was out dining with Swinburne. She 'lives on' only as the favourite model of the Brotherhood – a Viola here, a Sylvia there.

*

Deverell had discovered Elizabeth working in a milliner's shop off the Strand, and I am not exactly sure what this tragic tale of a shop assistant's death by painting has to do with my first meeting with Cawood Green – apart from a fatal alignment of bath tubs – although it does seem to me now that this set of associations is linked in some way to that song of his that I heard that night; somehow nudes and the ethics of craftsmanship have become entangled in my attempts to introduce the author of *Sinking* to you. Perhaps this is because my affiliation with Cawood Green is directly attributable to the fact that we continued our conversation that night largely because, on my side, a drugged and drowning woman slipping out of my fumbled reach was not, finally, much to go home to.

*

This, and Cawood Green coming to my professional aid when the club was failing in its sometime assistance in this regard, took us beyond our first chance contact. It was a Beginners' Night at the club that first night I heard him play, something I later learnt was rather ironic for Cawood Green. He had, in fact, been writing songs for years, but had always remained, as he put it, not so much a has-been as a never-was; he was quite comfortable with this – needed the anonymity, he claimed, to keep writing, although what the point was of the continued production of performance material when it was never really recognised in performance was beyond me. In any event, the reason I made it a habit to subject myself to Beginners' Nights was that there is nothing like some first attempts at song-writing to provide the worst sort of sentimentality available, and this is invaluable as potential material for one of my profession.

I am a writer of greeting card verse, a fact which should alert you to another reason as to why the concern with writing and morality that emerged from the accidental intersection of my tawdry daydreams and the E minor chord kept me in conversation with Cawood Green.

Knowledge of my profession should help you understand, too, why I have such trouble controlling this clumsy prose. I'm not used to sentences that go to the end of the line, or punctuation, capitals, dialogue (I'm going to drop trying to reproduce it from now on), all that sort of thing. I am, after all, a poet – of sorts; an occasional poet, if you like, one that packages the requisite emotions in *private words* that must be *addressed to you in public* on those standard occasions which punctuate our lives with the regularity of necessity – so, from my rather more materially gratifying anonymity, I reach out to an audience as well; in fact, I am intimately involved with a far greater volume of readers than your average poet – or unsuccessful songwriter, for that matter. Granted, one's collected works being displayed in supermarkets and newsagents under the categories of birthdays (family, general, year), anniversaries, congratulations, sympathy, thank you, and (my personal favourite as far as relationships are concerned) 'across the miles', doesn't carry with it the prestige of a Dewey number and library shelf, but I have made something of a name for myself in the industry with a rather important innovation.

While the company for which I work imports most of its material from an American conglomerate of which it is a subsidiary, I introduced the idea of nationalising the supposedly universal realm of sentimentality. Increasingly my work involved grafting images of the more exotic features of our country on to the standard occasions – zebra replaced reindeer, vast grasslands fields of snow, and so on. Collaborating with the artists, I, a failed one-time aspirant to their fraternity, have contributed in my way to William Burchell's appeal (made some thirty years before Guggums's ultimately fatal immersion in a setting exotic and alien to her actual circumstances) for a uniquely South African aesthetic schema – a vision to which South African artists in all fields have tried to give shape ever since (in order, usually, if they are white, to prove themselves less tourists in this landscape than Burchell himself). Unable to paint or draw, I have tried in my verse to generate pictures of my country that inspire not just the accommodation of the odd geographical reference, or some detail of flora or fauna, but the essence of a truly regional reaction to the common ceremonies that mark the stages of our lives – well, at least the lives of those in the social strata that observe the rituals for which we manufacture these devotional texts.

*

It is often-noted convention that the art produced by fictional artist figures in the works of which they are the protagonists remains absent from those works; there is something incommensurate between meditations on creating and the creating itself, it would seem. This is as good an excuse as any to spare you my verses, and explains why Cawood Green himself is not telling you the 'secret history' of his work. Perhaps it explains too, why so little of what I have to tell you has anything to do with *Sinking* itself; you must think of this history as a framing, as the foliage around its centre-piece, as the foreign setting which marks off the ordinary and turns it into art.

The mediations involved in these processes are never innocent and rarely to be trusted. Let's follow Guggums on her journey from the mundane to the tragic and back – that is, from store to studio to gallery to endless cheap reproductions. What happened to her as, through the potency of paint-stained hands running over her desperately unfamiliar Victorian shop-girl nakedness, she became that dying figure who is constantly revived by make-up, lighting, and costume? What was lost in her translation from the clumsy reality of tin bath, smoking lamps, costume jewellery, and second-hand gown to a realism so extreme it was only worthy of someone who never existed? What did it cost her to inhabit in the flesh a death which once was meant to exist only in the language of its report? How did it feel to be cut adrift by the edges of her picture from all the others in her story? What part was she allowed to play in her transubstantiation, she, the word become paint, losing her snatches of song in becoming visible? What honesty, or truth, or value is there in any of this?

And yet, if I could give my ghost voice such substance, fill her glass, warm her bath again and caress her lips, breasts, buttocks, shoulders, belly, cunt back into whatever poor semblance of life my art allowed, would I not die happy, and you not write books about me, my forgiven sins, my secret history?

*

Ophelia sang as she died – offstage, of course; on the night I met Cawood Green, a fifteen-year old on the stage singing her first composition – something to do with eyes, and rain, and misty window panes – brought about the slightly embarrassed revelation of my profession, and revealed Cawood Green's; in earning his living – no less than in the type of songs he has written and the places in which he performs them – he too, no surprise, exists like me in the strict material limits of South African middle-class life. Several beers and much defensive professional self-definition later (in which I laughingly had to admit to and dismiss my degree in Fine Arts), we had reached the shared confession of one of the standard fantasies of academics, journalists, librarians, bookshop employers and employees, advertising executives, even poets (and the creators of greeting card messages), that is, the intention of one day writing a novel. In response to my observation that anything I wrote in prose fell flatter than my most formulaic card verses, Cawood Green launched into what was obviously something of a set piece. I have heard him deliver it often enough since – and have looked up some of its references (although I promise you, no footnotes) – to be able to more or less re-create its general thrust. It is entitled

GENERIC INSTABILITY AND THE NATIONAL PROJECT

and begins with a challenge to poor old overused and usually misused Bakhtin's distinction between the 'monologic aspirations of the lyric' and the 'dialogic achievements of the novel'; *poetry behaves as if it lives in the heartland of its own language territory*, Cawood Green enjoys declaiming, contrasting this with the way in which the novel is an encyclopaedia of a whole range of its particular society's discourses.

Usually, he then goes on to make much of the relation between *the birth of the imagined community of the nation* and the novel form. This form, he claims, quoting Anderson, of course, *provided the technical means for 're-presenting' the kind of imagined community that is the nation*, providing a sense of a shared, simultaneous world in which one's relationship with others is guaranteed without first-hand knowledge or contact. Through the book (and the newspaper, as those familiar with the argument will remember), *fiction seeps quietly and continuously into reality, creating that remarkable confidence of community in anonymity which is the hallmark of modern nations.*

In South Africa, however, as Cawood Green has it, we have not managed to rise above competing exclusive nationalisms; lacking the necessary 'confidence of community', we do not have a convincing novel form. Cut off from the free-ranging dialogism available to writers with a guaranteed sense of community provided by a meaningful national identity, South Africans have always and only written 'poetry' in the strict sense defined by Bakhtin; trapped within our fractured and fragmented languages, we speak generically unstable monologues which constantly slip back into poetry, regardless of the external features of any form we use.

Therefore, he said with a flourish added in honour of my first exposure to his argument, not only should my greeting cards remain in verse – they only speak one language, and that of a particularly isolated enclave within the potential for nationhood all around us – but so should whatever writing we attempt (regardless of length or content, form, mode, or style) because our medium is always poetry. Just as the postal service only allows my birth/marriage/sympathy/etc. cards to circulate within a given and limited set of social conduits, so the aesthetics we practise is strictly contained within a self-defining and self-restricting set of communicative channels.

In his experience, Cawood Green concludes, our only recourse is to flaunt this state of affairs – the more overtly 'poetic' our work, the better, even when our (futile) aim is to produce a novel. This is the only strategy available to us until the medium in which we are trapped runs down or explodes, in either case allowing, eventually, for a collapse of the 'essences' (ethnicity, gender, class) of our time and place, and the development of modes of reciprocity (across, beyond, through the now-exposed constructedness of those essences) at present denied us.

*

Which should bring us, finally, to *Sinking*. At the time, however, I knew nothing of this work, which I was later to think of, despite his lecture, as Cawood Green's verse-novel; that night, Cawood Green's argument concerning poetry only brought forcefully home to me the monologues of two girls dying, each in their own isolated way, in their baths: the loneliness of Lizzie Siddal's dead-letters, poems that never found their way to us, ran like the edges of her drowned drawings into a medium from another time, a nameless voice ghosting out from electricity that was to become – through my failure to respond appropriately – not the occasion for an appropriate answer to its needs, but its own epitaph.

*

Now, having read *Sinking*, I'm not sure that these uncertain associations of loss (*a document in madness – thoughts and remembrance fitted*) are not truer to the kind of history Cawood Green wished to write than any recounting of his private history would have been. You have the 'poem', and what more is there to say about it, really? The Appendices add a bit, I suppose – anyway, they've become a part of the history of the poem; the story of *Sinking* pours into them and comes out the other end still itself, if not even a little

131

more so. The names of the authors of Appendices 2 and 4, pushed far enough, are the only clues we need to this – and, speaking of names, it's time for me to comment on 'Michael Cawood Green' – the name, that is, rather than the space it fills for readers unfamiliar with the writer in person.

The 'Cawood' is adopted, which means that he and I have in common not just the friendship that has occasioned his publisher's request for some personal background to his work, but our real names as well; indeed, we share this name with enough people of higher public profiles than ourselves to goad us into a common desire to either become better known than they – big enough, as Cawood Green once put it, so that when we shit, we miss nobody – or change our names. Cawood Green obviously opted for the latter, but in doing so is now well on the way to achieving the former (without evacuation, we all trust, but carry an umbrella at all times, anyway).

This is because, in a more serious vein, Cawood Green felt he had to be someone else in order to produce his first mature work. *Sinking* is in many ways driven by its author's earnest desire to avoid producing the Obligatory Autobiographical First Novel (Poem?). The adoption of 'Cawood' seems to have been a necessary step for Cawood Green in this regard. It is his mother's maiden name. She died when he was ten, and the true subject of any autobiographical work from Cawood Green would be the tension between his surnames – the closeness he felt to his mother, and the lack of identity with his father; the guilt associated with both: the unabsolved childhood sins against his mother, and the mixture of gratitude and distance he feels to the father who brought him up while the two of them were never able to communicate effectively; so, maternal emotional affiliation and loss, paternal material appreciation and resentment.

The domestic was not, of course, free of broader social categories. Cawood Green's father was, in South African terms, solidly lower middle-class – in any other country in which racial divides did not protect a certain status, working class; his mother, from genteel poverty – an old Settler family fallen on increasingly hard times as they followed the liberal cause in South Africa (grandfather Cawood, once an important figure in the United Party municipal authority of the Natal family seat, was marginalised after the electoral victory of the Nationalists). From this quasi-Lawrencian crucible came the typical driving mix of snobbism and sentimentality that results in the production of a form neither progenitor would appreciate – yet is motivated by the desire to placate them.

All this had to be cast into a time, place, and people distant enough to give Cawood Green a purchase on himself – hence the Sixties, Blyvooruitsig, the Oosthuizens; although he swears, in a romantic confession surprising in one of his critical persuasions, that he started to write *Sinking* purely because the first line surfaced of its own volition as he stood at the site of the disaster, and all the other voices demanded their respective says as the project took on a life of its own.

Well, in any event, he successfully found a subject to hide behind (something I'm very aware of failing to do here, despite the strategic alliances with a strange cast of associations I've been trying to assemble into some protective shape) and speak through; at least Cawood Green didn't make himself, as so many writers do when they write about themselves as artists, a painter.

*

For reasons that should be clear from the above he couldn't make himself a novelist either – although I can't resist another note on Cawood Green's choice of a middle name that may have also influenced him in his antagonism to the novel form: the only place the Cawood family have in South African literary history up to this point is the fact that, in essence, they fired (or at least refused to continue the tenure of) Olive Schreiner – because of her 'free-thinking' – from her position as tutor to their children; she was completing *The Story of an African Farm* at the time, and it is only a small comfort to Cawood Green that this seminal South African 'novel' is no such thing at all in his generic terms. This anecdote, in which the domestic, literary, and national intersect, is an irony Cawood Green does not so much appreciate as enact in his creative efforts.

*

Actually, there is yet another association with the name Cawood worth mentioning now that I've given up any pretence to order and form in this piece; no family history is complete without its skeleton, and a little digging into the Cawood's place of origin (so important in a colonial history) produces not just the requisite pile of bones but – and this should establish at least a vague relevance to its inclusion here – another drowning woman.

The Cawoods came to South Africa in 1820 from North Yorkshire; their founding fathers in the colonies, James, Joseph, and Joshua (sons of David Cawood), were all born in Yorkshire, and the family was old and important enough for a town in the region to be named after it. Cawood Castle was built on the site of King Athelstan's hall, and was originally the palace of the Archbishop of York (Cawood Green never forgave Shakespeare for not acknowledging in

Henry VIII that Wolsey was arrested there); it was fortified by Henry IV, and reduced to ruin – except for the gatehouse (now a private property) – in the Civil War.

Less dramatically, in historical terms at least, it was also the setting for a ghost story – a documented one, accepted as fact by the York assizes in 1690, and used as grounds for a conviction in a murder case – which makes it a detective story too. If the historian may best be described as a ghost-hunting detective, then this incidental anecdote may serve as a clue to the essence of the activity expressed in *Sinking*; the fact that it is based on a 'true story' (a key recommendation in the popularity of many a fantastic best-seller) reinforces the significance that pure coincidence can manufacture when one allows history the play of its full facticity.

*

William Barwick arrived late on the night of 14 April at the house of his brother-in-law, Thomas Lofthouse, to announce that his wife had left for her uncle's house in Selby. This was readily believed, as it was no secret that William and Mary Barwick did not get on well together and quarrelled frequently; 'but Heaven would not be so deluded', John Aubrey tells us in his *Miscellanies*, continuing:

> and raised up the ghost of the murdered woman to make the discovery. And therefore it was upon the Easter Tuesday following, about two of the clock in the afternoon, the forementioned Lofthouse having occasion to water a quickset hedge, not far from his house; as he was going for the second pail full, an apparition went before him in the shape of a woman, and soon after sat down upon a rising green grass-

plot, right over against the pond; he walked by her as he went to the pond, and as he returned with the pail from the pond, looking sideways to see whether she continued in the same place, he found she did . . . So soon as he had emptied his pail, he went into his yard, and stood still to try whether he could see her again, but she was vanished.

In this information he says, that the woman seemed to be habited in a brown coloured petticoat, waistcoat, and a white hood; such a one as his wife's sister usually wore, and that her countenance looked extremely pale and wan, with her teeth in sight, but no gums appearing, and that her physiognomy was like to that of his wife's sister, who was wife to William Barwick.

Shaken and suspicious, Lofthouse shared this experience with his wife; they went to the uncle in Selby, found no trace of Mary's having been there, and reported their fears to the Lord Mayor of York. A warrant of arrest was made out for Barwick, who at first changed his story to one of having sold his wife for five shillings, but eventually made the following statement:

The examination of William Barwick, taken the twenty-fifth day of April, 1690. WHO sayeth and confesseth, that he carried his wife over a certain wain-bridge, called Bishopdike-bridge, betwixt Cawood and Sherborne, and within a lane about one hundred yards from the said bridge, and on the left hand of the said bridge, he and he wife went over a stile, on the left hand of a certain gate, entering into a certain close on the left hand of the said lane; and in a pond in the said close, adjoining to a quickwood-hedge, did drown his wife, and upon the bank of the said pond, did bury her; and further, that he was within sight of Cawood Castle, on the left hand; and that there was but one hedge betwixt the said close, where he drowned his said wife, and the Bishopslates belonging to the said castle.

The dense detail of this confession – probably read back into a less geographically-exact account after being extracted in pursuit of evidence – led to the discovery of the victim's corpse and the execution of the murderer, whose 'body was left hanging in chains as a dreadful warning'.

*

Cawood Green had come across this case while investigating his Settler affiliations, and was disturbed by the fact that, while on study leave in England (and before being aware of the Barwick story), he had taken a picture of his wife – scenically surrounded by a Yorkshire summer's lush array of reeds, moss, and flowers (*crow-flowers, nettles, daisies, and long purples*) – standing next to a pond in Cawood, with the Castle's gatehouse in the background.

*

Why is it that ghosts are our surest guides to mark our way? – that, despite our best efforts to drive them to pills and alcohol, dress them in garments that will pull them to a muddy death, or to hold their heads under stagnant water until the bubbles cease, they rise from the mists of where we bury them, and walk with us, edging us along (more surely than those living, breathing, substantial companions we preserve from our murderous thoughts) in directions we think we choose? It is not the historian who is the detective, rooting out history's secrets – it is the past which follows every clue to its logical conclusion, making itself visible in the absence of our confessions, forcing us to know ourselves in our very making.

*

The fact that *Sinking* was written in the final year of Cawood Green's collapsing marriage may explain some of the enormous sense of loss the story exudes. His wife's family live in the Far West Rand, and it was while on a visit to them that he discovered the story and location of the disaster, dimly remembered from his childhood, at a mine near Carletonville.

The fact, too, that *Sinking* was written in the same year in which South Africa celebrated its first democratic elections, the year in which a fledgeling inclusive nationalism fluttered out of the shadow of a clash of competing exclusive nationalisms (excuse me, I am a writer of greeting cards, not social history), brings the features of domestic collapse and political rebirth into an obvious alignment; in the years leading up to these events, many artists – especially those isolated by their social positioning from mass action – were concerned with forging in their art bonds between the personal and the national, creating there connections they were all too rarely able to find in their lives.

Interestingly, the combining of the private and the political was at the centre of what Cawood Green (then simply Mike Green) had tried to achieve as a songwriter. I include here the lyrics of some of Cawood Green's songs –

most of which I heard him perform on various occasions –
to show how the early clear separation between romantic
ballads and aggressive political material began to blur in
the more mature work.

*

SUPPLEMENT: SONGS

Is it All History Now?

Or, What Did You Do in the War, Daddy?

You must sing 'A-down, a-down';
and you 'Call him a-down-a'.

1:   THE SOLDIER'S GOT A NAME
(Pinetown, 1973/*Durban, 1989*)

The pigeons in the park have shat
Upon the people in stone fame,
The kings and queens and conquerors
And the soldier with no name;

And on this wind-blown hillside
The crosses just stretch for miles,
Small and plain, each one just the same,
They crown their crumbling piles.

And we are left to carry on with the game of history,
Egged on by words like pride and right and necessity;
Are they just words? They echo absurd
In the wind among the graves . . .

Now we've all raised our hands and killed
Our sons for the vision we've seen,
But up here on this hillside
It's just a faded dream;

And all those black-edged telegrams
That lie dusty in old drawers,
They're just receipts for paying a price too high
To win some nameless war.

And we are left to carry on with the game of history,
Egged on by words like race and class and nationality;
Are they just words? They echo absurd
In the wind among the graves . . .

And if Edendale is burning
It's no angel with a flaming sword,
It's guns and knives and necklaces
That make up this fallen world;

And for those who go recruiting
Children in the night
To strip their clothes and tear their flesh,
Goodnight, comrades, goodnight . . .

And we are left to carry on with the game of history,
Egged on by words like Inkatha, MK, and ANC;
Are they just words? They echo absurd
In the wind among the graves . . .

So keep the home fire burning
Though our children won't come home again,
And by its flame and their dear names
Let's swear to live for life again.

2:   **THREE VERSES FOR M.**
    (Stanford, 1978)

I've wandered down these ruins of time about as far as I
    plan to go,
I've heard one set of footsteps enough to know I'm on my
    own;
I've been fooled by ghosts and echoes of hope once too
    often in the night,
Standing on a windy corner watching your fading
    bedroom light.

And it's hard to keep cross the empty miles, it's hard to
    cross the sea;
But it's harder still to break your heart each night and
    know it never bleeds.

Well there's a tale on every corner, where all streets meet
    and part,
Secret loves with initialled hopes and an arrow through
    each heart;
And I wrote them down and I learned each one and sang
    them as best I could,
But I watched them fade until the only trace was a lost
    heart carved in wood.

And it's hard to keep a memory while the future drowns
    each day,

But it's harder still to let the past go free, when you know
    it won't go away . . .
And I can still see your face half-lit by the glow of the
    dashboard lights,
As you slept beside me hidden from the storm-swept
    highway night;
Between the headlights and the windscreen wipers I
    could hardly see my way,
And I felt betrayed by your half-smiling sleep, but I
wanted it this way.

Yes it's hard to put your foot right down, close your eyes
    and let go of the wheel,
But it's harder still to drive on into a night where
    nothing is revealed . . .

3:   JOHN VORSTER SQUARE
(Stanford, 1979)

It's rush hour in Johannesburg, cars jam the main
    thoroughfare,
A river of humanity flows past John Vorster Square;
Thirteen storeys the building stands but for anyone who
    cares'
There are a thousand stories to break your heart in John
    Vorster Square.

The laws are harsh in a land where peace is kept by
    suppression
And John Vorster Square waits for you if you're suspected
    of transgression;
The top two floors are barred and sound-proofed so you
    can't call for a trial that's fair,
Anyway they don't need a courtroom to keep you in John
    Vorster Square.

Daniel raised his voice at Soweto so he was put away,
His friends all came to John Vorster Square and knelt
    outside to pray;
But their prayer was broken by a baton charge, accused of
    attacking on their knees,
One hundred and forty six students learned John Vorster
    Square hears no pleas.

On the city streets you can hear detainees singing from
their cells,
And the words the wind carries to you speak of a living,
dying hell;
Songs of torture and suicide and exits besides the stairs,
Because some have just fallen ten floors from John
Vorster Square.

Wellington Tshazibane went to Oxford from Fort Hare,
But a brilliant academic record couldn't keep him from
John Vorster Square;
They tell us he hanged himself in his cell, but his body
bears the scars
Of the type of justice one can expect behind John
Vorster's bars.

All these crimes in the name of justice, in whose name do
you dare
To break the law in the name of the law in John Vorster
Square?
And all those ghosts both dead and alive, they ask you
now in pain
John Vorster are you proud to have that building bear
your name?

4:   BERLIN, 1931
       (Tulare, 1979/Johannesburg, 1980)

I met you in Berlin, it was 1931;
You had green finger nails, you were not the only one,
Do you remember a place, do you remember a time?
There was music and laughter, the saddest of each
    kind . . .

You sang in a show, I sat in a chair,
A bubble of spotlight held you in the champagne air,
Do you remember a time, do you remember a place?
There's no more eye-shadow, but I remember your face.

I met you in Berlin, it was 1931,
Our friends were all dying, the night came for the young;
You ordered something, it came on a tray
And the waiter was faceless, as he took the death's-head
    away . . .

I met you in Berlin, it was 1931,
The city was grey, the steel-grey of a gun;
You danced for them naked – you were white with black
    eyes,
And the café was crowded as you took them alive;

Do you remember a swastika on our bedroom wall?
Do you remember it well? Do you remember it at all?

We hung your dress over it, the one edged in lace,
You're not naked now, but I remember your face.

I met you in Berlin, it was 1931,
Do you remember a cabaret, and the smoke in your
    lungs?
I wore a great-coat and you wore a smile,
And we were the jury for a nation on trial;

I met you in Berlin, it was 1931,
Our friends were all dying, the night came for the young;
You ordered something, it came on a tray
And the waiter was faceless, as he took the death's-head
    away . . .

5: AN OLD SOUTH AFRICAN LOVE SONG, OR, SARIE MARAIS REVISITED

(Johannesburg, 1984)

Now you know why it's so warm in bed together,
Look around you the house is burning down;
I don't think this is what they had in mind when they
    sang about the home fires burning,
But it looks like it's really caught on in this town.
Turn away from the mirror to the window,
Oh, come on do you even have to ask?
You can't really believe we've got problems of a serious
    nature,
After all, we're armed, white, and middle class.

Or do you think those men in camouflage aren't out there
    for you?
Attack or protection, there's a thin line running through.
Moustaches under peaked caps, looking vaguely bored,
Judges studying stains on the ground
That just aren't a metaphor for anything any more . . .

Listening for the freedom songs in the distance
You hear the wind in the wire and the sentinel's cough,
A soldier holds an automatic weapon like a child in his
    arms,
A guard dog barks somewhere not far off;
And somewhere out there there's a boy dreaming he's on
    commando,

Singing 'Sarie Marais' out on some windy plain;
An armoured machine rumbles by and he starts and he
    wakes and he thinks,
Sarie, why are you looking at me that way?
Sarie, why are you looking at me that way?

6: LILI MARLEEN (AGAIN)
(Johannesburg, 1984)

Lili Marleen is standing in the rain by a street light,
Her hair is a halo, it's just the light and shadow of a wet
     night;
In her lips a cigarette, is she trying to forget a song sung
     in World War Two?
She blows another smoke-ring and then she crushes
     something under her little shoe . . .

And you know I've tried that raincoat, with the hat down
     over my eyes,
I'm just a valve-radio detective who can't see through his
     own disguise;
Don't you know I've tried . . . oooo, I've tried.

All the usual boys with their old-fashioned ploys are out
     tonight,
Looking for Lili in the heat of the city with their maps
     and search-lights;
Some went to war for the one they adored, I heard it on
     the radio,
That they're not coming back and Lily's so sad that she's
     cancelled the show . . .

And you know I've tried that raincoat, with the hat down
     over my eyes,

I'm just a valve-radio detective who can't see through his
   own disguise;
Don't you know I've tried . . . oooo, I've tried.

Now Lili Marleen is still standing in the rain by a street
   light,
In her hands a dead-letter, no he didn't forget her the
   night he died;
In her lips a cigarette, is she trying to forget a song about
   World War Two?
She rereads the ending and then she crushes something
   under her little shoe . . .

And you know I've tried that raincoat, with the hat down
   over my eyes,
I'm just a valve-radio detective who can't see through his
   own disguise;
Don't you know I've tried . . . oooo, I've tried.

7:   CASUAL VIOLENCE
   (Durban, 1989)

Mist on the mountain, smoke in the sky,
It's another day in Eden and two more people have to die,
And the sins of the children find their way straight to
    their parents' heads;
Such casual violence, I just can't take any more,
It's in the name of the people, but do we know who they
    are any more?

The morning sun is purple, it catches blood on the grass,
Cold bodies lie where laughing school children pass,
And a peace-keeping soldier grips his gun and he just
    stares;
Such casual violence, I just can't take any more,
It's in the name of the people, but do we know who they
    are any more?

A child goes to school so he has to hide from his home,
Lives with his grandmother 'til the crowd finds her alone,
Then it's pangas and matches, she's old so it doesn't take
    very long;
Such casual violence, I just can't take any more,
It's in the name of the people, but do we know who they
    are any more?

There's no such thing as a vacuum, especially when it
    comes to power,

In a community deprived of law the most gorgeous
    warlords flower,
And poverty feeds hunger until you'll kill just for access
    to a tap;
Such casual violence, I just can't take any more,
It's in the name of the people, but do we know who they
    are any more?

There are no heroes in anarchy, no sides to choose,
It's kill or be killed, but on all sides you lose;
Just as it finds itself this nation tears itself apart;
Such casual violence, I just can't take any more,
It's in the name of the people, but do we know who they
    are any more?

8:   HEROINE GOES HOME, BLEEDING
      (Johannesburg, 1988/Durban, 1993)

There's a storm just over the horizon
Bleeding into the night,
It'll catch us before morning,
You're still sleeping, well sleep tight . . .

You've got your promises and I've got my pride,
Between the two this is suicide;
In the dark I lie and watch you breathe,
In the morning we'll wake and watch each other bleed;

Because you're just another wounded soldier
For me to comfort 'til you ride
Out into the wasteland you loved until they blew you
      open wide;
You're just a casualty, another refugee,
You're no longer free, but you'll make history,
And leave us on our own . . .

Were you burned on the wing running on the wind
Did you see who got you or even what happened?
As you fell into the spin that took you down
Did you enjoy the ride just one last time?

And now there's not even ashes where you burned out,
Just a total eclipse and the morning fallout –
And it's just as well you're not around
Because styles have changed, they'd want you underground;

And I'm wondering where you'll find the faith and
     certainty
To step outside believing you are free,
The lines are down, the roads are blocked,
And your name's on the radio –
You're just a casualty, another refugee,
You're no longer free, but you'll make history,
And leave us on our own . . .

Well, the street's not the same since you embraced your
     fall,
Although some still remember, I saw your name on a
     wall,
The paint was red and the letters had run,
You bled like a martyr, just like anyone;

But we don't need dead saints in the heart of the storm,
We don't need prayers or ghosts in uniform,
We need strong hands to win the fight,
We need another leader, lover in the night:

We lie here in fear of the knock on the door,
I love you and hate you for losing the war,
You were our heroine, our Joan of Arc,
But now you're bleeding beside me in the dark;
You're just a casualty, another refugee,
You're no longer free, but you'll make history,
And leave us on our own . . .

9: UNTITLED
(Durban, 1995)

Lights on the water, there's a small craft warning out tonight,
Here on the Esplanade, safe from the wind, I feel all right;
I never was a sailor, never had the legs to walk those
    waves alone,
So I'll just sit here next to the statue of Dick King as he
    rides by for help, carved in stone

And it's a long, long way,
It's a long way to go back in time
To the days, the days before I served my sentence
Or even committed my crime,
And this town was young,
At least it felt that way,
Is it just me,
Or is it just yesterday
That let us laugh and let us play
In this city of heartbreak?

And I'm going to go walking with you on my arm through
    the shadows of Newton's Fun Fare;
Got on the ghost train one night, someone turned out the
    lights, now it's no longer there;
We won so many prizes from people with the saddest
    faces I've ever seen,
Sick from the rides with you laughing in your candy
    floss, I shot up everything
And it's a long, long way . . .

And I remember when even if you were white you could
    go to the Blue Lagoon,
Eat chips off a tray attached to the window of your car,
    drink a milkshake too,
Then walk down onto the beach where the foam grew
    luminous as you escaped the floodlights,
Make love on the sand – I can still see your breasts, white
    in the moonlight
And it's a long, long way . . .

When you were hungry at 2 a.m. it was the Cuban Hat,
Gazing out at Addington Beach from under its brim, that
    beach just stared back;
And I remember when I was eleven a toy soldier lost and
    mourned on the battlefield,
While behind me in the hospital, cancer made sure my
    mother's lips were sealed
And it's a long, long way . . .

The Fairhaven hotel hangs a red circle in the coke-black
    sky,
Stars bubbled off your skin as we waited in the night heat
    to go inside;
And there there was a microphone we'd use to fill the air
    with the certainty of being right,
Yes, we'd play out our hearts for chicken à la king, Castle
    beer, and a place in the spotlight
And it's a long, long way . . .

I had these friends, they went into exile in Amsterdam
And they had a child there conceived in this city they
    wanted to grow up a free man;
So they called him Tegwen after this place they were so
    desperately missing,
And I've never had the heart to tell them 'Tegwen' means
    one-testicled thing
And it's a long, long way . . .

Can you see those wooden ships floating out there just
    beyond the waves
Staring at us invisible on some future shore on some
    other Christmas day?
What birth did they bring, what children are we of their
    shipwrecks?
They gave us a name, put us on the map, and then they
    just left
And it's a long, long way,

It's a long way to go back in time
To the days, the days before I served my sentence
Or even committed my crime,
And this town was young,
At least it felt that way,
Is it just me,
Or is it just yesterday
That let us laugh and let us play
In this city of heartbreak?

*

161

Hopefully these songs will tell you something about the work featured in this publication – more, at least, than the tenuous connections I have with its author allow me, or my even more tenuous attempts to register how past meets present in the most accidental alignments of his text and the space in which I read it. Most of *Sinking*'s history must remain secret, as far as I am concerned, but if anything emerges from the choreographed collisions I have put before you, it must be that it is not just an author, a family, or a nation going down in that story. There are obviously more ways than one to go to ground, just as there are so many ways to drown – in a bath, a pond, or a river, or even in history itself; but this flow of forced and inexact associations is drying up – *too much of water hast thou, poor Ophelia*, and I must let you be.

*

Let me end by saying that I went home, that night after first meeting Cawood Green, to find a couple of messages on my answering machine. The first was from Constable Kawula, letting me know they had had no luck in tracing my ghost voice. The second was from my ex-wife, telling me that the phone had rung while she was in the bath, and at the instant, naked and dripping, she'd picked up the receiver, it had gone dead; had I called? – she hated not knowing who it was she'd missed.

*

There was no third call, the only one in which I was really interested: a voice – coming out of the depths of some loss too big to ever fill, or from the even more painful heights of a hope all the more necessary for being beyond fulfilment –

telling me how to say, meaningfully, convincingly, in the clarity and simplicity of the prose of the perfect greeting card, that, whatever the occasion, it's all going to be . . .

. . . and here is a vital element of the historical that we have avoided until now, but can no longer: *the future* – oh, I wish I could say to you that it's all really, really going to be . . .

. . . can I say it? Is it so difficult to say because narrative tends to keep us in the past tense, regardless of deictics; a story, after all, represents all experience linguistically as *past* experience, if only because of the rupture between the moment of narration and the narrative evoked. Does this make not only, as the old cliché would have it, all history story, but all story history?

My card verses, on the other hand, hold me in the present moment, and are so easily disposable for this very reason; no history, only nostalgia. And poetry, as that ancient and somewhat tired urn reminds us, is for the for-ever now – no transition from one state to another, and so no history in the achieved form, no matter how much history drowns that form.

Well, that gives us two hands full, so how do we find a purchase on the future? In the deep secrets of grammar, of course, in the *secret systems* where no less a *network of levels and pressures* sustains us than in the uncertain ground upon which Cawood Green built his story – for the grammatical mood of a story does not necessarily reflect the actual manner of its assertions, and narrative tense is not a sufficient indicator of the temporal situation being treated. In this lies our only hope, for here we go beyond the present of poetry, the past of history. We must learn to live in the implied subjunctive of the utopian mode, which, despite its surface grammatical tense (past) and mood (indicative), is ruled by the future tense and the subjunctive mood. This is the grammar of desire, which reverberates through chunks of prose flung down in a single, huge chord in which the tension builds, setting the separate strands of a story quivering, vibrating, dancing in unison – until a vase upon its pedestal, full of flowers collected in the wake of a singing, sinking woman, shatters from within, and its pieces are gathered up from amongst the petals, and become what we hold holy in our procession, facing backwards, towards the . . .

. . . and I *want*, oh I want so much to say to you in that ideal greeting card suitable for all the occasions thrown up by history, a card posted from somewhere not too far before us, that, yes,

Lizzie with your laudanum,
Hettie with your sea,
Marianne with your mother,
Martha with your victory;
Jannie with your hands,
Delene with your name,
Four wives with your husband,
Ophelia with your frame;
Michael with your two names,
Johannes with your water,
Karl with your comedy,
Ghost voice with your answer

it's all going to be, despite everything that's gone before, despite the moment in which I write this, despite everything which is for us ever *afterwards*, it's all going to be
— all right.

*

There's rosemary, that's for remembrance.
Pray, love, remember.